Milo March is a hard-drinking, womanizing, wisecracking, James-Bondian character. He always comes out on top through a combination of personality, bluff, bravado, luck, skill, experience, and intellect. He is a shrewd judge of human character, a crack shot, and a deeper character than I have found in most of the other spy/thriller novels I've read. But, above all, he is a con-man—and a very good one. It is Milo March himself who makes the series worth reading.

—Don Miller, *The Mystery Nook* fanzine 12

Steeger Books is proud to reissue twenty-three vintage novels and stories by M.E. Chaber, whose Milo March Mysteries deliver mile-a-minute action and breezily readable entertainment for thriller buffs.

Milo is an Insurance Investigator who takes on the tough cases. Organized crime, grand theft, arson, suspicious disappearances, murders, and millions and millions of dollars—whatever it is, Milo is just the man for the job. Or even the only man for it.

During World War II, Milo was assigned to the OSS and later the CIA. Now in the Army Reserves, with the rank of Major, he is recalled for special jobs behind the Iron Curtain. As an agent, he chops necks, trusses men like chickens to steal their uniforms, shoots point blank at secret police—yet shows compassion to an agent from the other side.

Whatever Milo does, he knows how to do it right. When the work is completed, he returns to his favorite things: women, booze, and good food, more or less in that order....

THE MILO MARCH MYSTERIES

Hangman's Harvest

No Grave for March

The Man Inside

As Old as Cain

The Splintered Man

A Lonely Walk

The Gallows Garden

A Hearse of Another Color

So Dead the Rose

Jade for a Lady

Softly in the Night

Uneasy Lies the Dead

Six Who Ran

Wanted: Dead Men

The Day It Rained Diamonds

A Man in the Middle

Wild Midnight Falls

The Flaming Man

Green Grow the Graves

The Bonded Dead

Born to Be Hanged

Death to the Brides

The Twisted Trap: Six Milo March Stories

Born to Be Hanged

KENDELL FOSTER CROSSEN
Writing as
M.E. CHABER

STEEGER BOOKS / **2021**

PUBLISHED BY STEEGER BOOKS
Visit steegerbooks.com for more books like this.

©2001, 2021 by Kendra Crossen Burroughs
The unabridged novel has been edited by Kendra Crossen Burroughs.

First Paperback Edition

PUBLISHING HISTORY

Hardcover
New York: Holt, Rinehart & Winston (A Rinehart Suspense Novel), August 1973. Dust jacket by Jay Smith.
Toronto: Holt, Rinehart & Winston of Canada, August 1973.
Roslyn, NY: Detective Book Club #379, Walter J. Black, Inc., November 1973. (With *Reckless Lady* by Rae Foley and *Conquest before Autumn* by Matthew Eden.)

ISBN: 978-1-61827-583-7

For Marcelia

She walks in the early morning like a rose
Lifting its petals to greet the dawn,
Each petal the warm ruby of a midnight kiss,
Lifting eagerly for the caress of the golden fingers
Reaching from the soft blue backdrop of the day.
Looking upward and beyond, before they meet,
She says good-bye to the last lingering star.

—Stefan Krosno

CONTENTS

9 / Born to Be Hanged

241 / A Last Goodbye

247 / About the Author

ONE

The rays of the sun reached through the office windows and covered the walls with yellow finger painting. But it was the only thing to enter the office. Every morning had been like that for a month. I was tired of it. I had finished reading the morning paper, including the reports of baseball spring training. I opened a desk drawer and took out a bottle of brandy. I poured a small drink and sipped it. I was thinking of going out, locking the door, and doing something exciting—like taking a walk in Central Park.

The phone rang. I picked up the receiver. "March's Agency," I said. That's me. I'm Milo March. I'm also the agency.

"Milo, boy, how are you?" It was Martin Raymond. He's a vice-president of Intercontinental Insurance, the company I do most of my work for. I was about to tell him that I wasn't sure I was up to visiting a rarefied atmosphere so early in the morning, but then I remembered that he's the one that hands out all of those jobs. Every time he calls me, I hear the counting of money. It always sounds like crisp lettuce.

"I haven't checked with my doctor yet," I said. "I've been sitting here counting the minutes and wondering if I would ever again hear the sound of a friendly voice—and then you called. I must be a … is it psychic or psycho? I can never remember."

Martin Raymond was never sure how he was supposed to react, but he dutifully made a noise that sounded more like a whinny than a laugh. I had to at least give him credit for trying.

"Are you busy?" he asked.

"That's a good question," I said. "I was sitting here wondering whether I should go on being busy or take a nice walk in Central Park. They tell me that's where the action is."

This time he didn't even try to laugh. That was a sign that he was about to get down to business. "I think we might have a small job for you," he said. That meant that he was hoping I wouldn't take too many days on it because I cost three hundred dollars for each day. Plus expenses.

"If it's that small," I said, "why don't you turn it over to one of the office boys? Give him a fat expense account, and I'll give him the name and address of a good bar. All he has to do is mention my name and he can get dry martinis for a dollar and a half a clip. That should result in an imaginative report. A little editing and you could probably submit it for a Pulitzer Prize. In fiction."

"We tried that once with one of your expense accounts, but they said that it was too amateurish." He sounded pleased with what he considered a bit of humor.

"Please," I said with a pained sound. "I'm supposed to make the jokes around here. Besides, if you think my expense accounts are amateurish, I don't want to hear any more complaints about them being padded."

That was supposed to be a mortal blow, but he ignored it. "If you're not too busy," he said, returning to the friendly-but-executive level, "why not drop in and we'll run over the case?"

"I forgot to bring my parachute," I said, "but I'll stroll up and see you. Maybe we can run it up a flagpole and see whose anthem is played first." On that cheerful note, I hung up.

I lit a cigarette and finished my small drink. Then I shrugged into my jacket and left. It was a short walk up Madison Avenue to the concrete-and-glass building which stood as a monument to the enforced generosity of the policyholders of Intercontinental Insurance.

The executive offices were high up in the building. It was from there that I was dispatched to various parts of the world to toil in the Intercontinental vineyards. I am their chief investigator, which means that if you try to cut corners in order to collect the face value of your insurance policy, I am supposed to uncover the corners. At the risk of life and limb. For three hundred dollars a day and expenses. This also explains why they take a negative attitude toward selling me a large amount of insurance.

I stepped out of the elevator into the reception room. I stopped to admire the girl who was busy at the desk. She was something to look at. She had long black hair, large black eyes, a smooth Latin complexion, and full pouting lips. The rest of her was just as lovely. Her accessories were ample enough to stop the traffic on any street. She walked like a miracle on the way to happening.

Her name was Carmen O'Brien, the result of an Irish father and a Latin American mother. I had taken her to dinner several times, and she was always fun to be with. I had only one complaint. She had a roommate who was always there reading a book whenever I took Carmen home. It was enough to make a man lose his faith in American apple pie.

I walked over to the desk. She looked up just as I reached it. Her smile was like the first glimpse of the morning sun.

"Hello, Milo," she said.

"Hello," I answered. "I know I've seen you somewhere before. Now, let me think."

She laughed. "Do you want to see Mr. Raymond?"

"I don't want to. I am forced to by circumstances beyond my control. Namely, my bank account."

She picked up her phone and dialed three numbers. She said my name, waited, and hung up. "Go right in," she said. That meant Martin Raymond had already told his secretary to have me come in as soon as I arrived.

I went through a door. I started walking down the long strip of thick carpeting that led to his office. I always thought of it as the Last Mile.*

His secretary looked up as I reached her desk. "Well, if it isn't the boy wonder himself. He said to send you right in. His voice sounded like an alert signal, so I went down and told the cashier to lock her cage until further notice."

"If I'm questioned about it," I said, "I'll say that I always spend half of my expense money on you."

"I'll bet you would. You'd better go on in. He's being nervous today."

"What's up?" I asked.

"I don't know. But I believe he's been thinking all morning. I've even heard him pacing several times."

"That is bad. I hope he hasn't done too much thinking. He's

---

* In the sense of a condemned man's walk to the place of execution. (All footnotes were added by the editor.)

not built for it. He's liable to be incoherent by the time I reach him. See you on the way out, honey."

I walked past her and opened the door. He was sitting at his desk, his fingers drumming on the blotter. He looked up as I closed the door behind me.

"There you are," he said, sounding like a man who had just discovered that the sun rises every morning. He waved across the room. "Help yourself to a drink. You know where the bar is."

"I thought you'd never ask," I murmured. I walked over to an antique cabinet. It probably had once been very valuable, but he'd had it changed so that it was now a complete bar. I poured myself a healthy drink of bourbon, dropped in a couple of ice cubes, and then crossed to a chair beside his desk.

"I take it," I said, "that some vulgarian has dipped his unclean hand into the family till?"

"Two million dollars," he said grimly.

"That's grand larceny," I said.

"Fraud," he said. "Barefaced fraud. They'll never get away with it. We'll stop them in their tracks."

"We?" I asked. "I think I just felt an angel tap me on my shoulder."

He lifted his head and stared at me as if seeing me for the first time. "Milo, my boy, you're just the man for the job."

"That was a fast promotion from boy to man," I said gently. "Are you going to tell me about the case, or do I have to guess?"

"What?" he asked. Then his expression changed as he got

the message. "Yes. Of course." He cleared his throat. "Did you ever hear of Reno, Nevada?"

"I seem to remember such a place," I said dryly. "The Biggest Little City in the World. I think that's what it's called. What have you been doing, insuring a bunch of casino players?"

"This is no time for jokes," he said seriously. "About six months ago we issued a policy for two million dollars on a gold mine not far from Reno."

"Two million dollars on an old abandoned gold mine?* You must have had gold dust in your eyes."

"Not at all," he said with dignity. "We had it completely checked out."

"Of course," I said. "Then it just happened to go dry within six months. Or maybe they had a hot, dry spell and all the pretty gold just melted and ran away. I've heard of Renoites who bragged about the local water, but I never heard of the water containing gold. They must have salted it."

"Salted it? What does that mean?"

"Putting gold where there never was any gold before. I don't know how it's done in this modern age but in the old days it was done by loading a shotgun with gold and then firing several loads around in the area where the digging was going on."

"Nothing like that could have happened in this case," he said. "We had some sample ore assayed and the report stated

---

* The author's interest in mining as a plot element goes way back. In radio days, he wrote the script "The Saint Goes Underground" (December 17, 1947), in which the Saint gets involved with a Nevada mine that is supposedly worthless but upon investigation is found to be full of a valuable mineral.

that the gold content was very high. We also hired an expert to go into the mine and give us a report on it. He did and said that there was the beginning of a very rich vein where they had recently started digging."

"Handling all of this from here by mail, I suppose?"

"Not at all. We had one of our men go out and get those things done, and also talk to various people in the vicinity. All of the reports were excellent. In fact, the investigator brought this back with him." He indicated a large rock on his desk, serving as a paperweight.

"Pyrites of Iron?" I asked.

"What's that?"

"It's also known as Fool's Gold. It's about all you find if you go around peering under toadstools. Or in old abandoned gold mines. There is nothing to indicate that a mine was ever abandoned because there was too much gold in it."

"You might be interested to learn," he said coldly, "that our expert estimated that there was a minimum of between four and five million dollars' worth of gold in that mine."

"Interesting," I said. "Did you ever read anything by Robert Service?"

"Who'd he work for?"

"For himself. Just like me. He was a poet."

"Never read the stuff," he said proudly. "What did he have to say that has anything to do with this?"

"He had quite a bit to say about gold. In fact, he said one thing that reminds me of the tone of voice you used when you announced how much gold there is in that mine. In a poem about gold and men, he wrote:

"The waves have a story to tell me ...

Of men who sally in quest of gold

To sink in an ocean grave."

"Milo, my boy," he said seriously, "there are times when I worry about you. Are you sure you're feeling all right?"

"I think so. I think you mentioned something about two million dollars?"

"Yes, yes. It's that case in Reno, Nevada. Two million dollars is the face value of the policy. They're demanding full payment. We're depending on you, Milo."

"Don't you always?" I lit a cigarette and took another sip of the bourbon. "You did mention that you issued an insurance policy for two million dollars. If the mine ran out of gold, you are to pay them two million dollars?"

"That's right. You're getting the picture, Milo."

I leaned back and laughed. "That's the funniest thing you've ever said, Martin. Why did you issue the policy?"

"Because there was gold there. Our assayer estimated that it would be well over four million dollars, depending on how long the vein runs."

"You hired the assayer yourself?"

"Well, not personally," he said evasively. "Bracken checked on him and gave me all the information. I told Bracken to hire him and have him bill us."

I got up and poured myself another drink. "Did this assayer have a name?"

"Of course. It's Manfred Smith. He's been an assayer most of his life. Much of the new activity in both silver and gold in Nevada has resulted from his reports."

"That's nice. What does he charge for his good news?"

"He charges the same whether the news is good or bad. Five hundred dollars for the report."

"Not bad," I said dryly, "if he gets enough orders. Who's this Bracken you mentioned?"

"One of our staff investigators. He went to Reno and conducted the investigations."

"Been with you long?"

"About ten years. A good man. He handles most of the investigation done before we issue a policy."

"Is that why I have to bail you out so often when it looks as if you're going to have to pay face value?"

He made an impatient gesture. Martin Raymond didn't like to be questioned by the help. "We can't expect to be right every time. Some of the crooks are pretty damn smart. You know that."

"Yeah. What about this Bracken? Do you think he might be tempted to tell you what you wanted to hear? For a price, naturally."

"Impossible. I told you he's been with us for years. We trust him implicitly. Of course, he's checked out every year."

"Of course," I said mildly. "By the way, Martin, old friend, do you also check me out every year?"

He gave me a thin-lipped smile which showed more of his character than his usual relaxed grin. "Of course. You must have known that it was done. You've been around."

"I've been around long enough to smell things like that," I said. "Now, who owns this little mine and is now presenting you with a little bill for two million pieces of green?"

"It's owned by a corporation. Three owners. But I don't have to tell you all this. I had my girl type out all of the essential information, and she'll give it to you on the way out. With your expense money."

"How much?"

"Two thousand dollars. That ought to last you long enough to clean this up. We have every confidence in you, Milo, my boy." His good humor was returning.

"You're all heart, Martin," I murmured, "but you're overlooking one thing. I haven't yet said that I would take the job."

"What?" he said. It was almost a shout, and he once more looked the part of a harassed executive. "Our agreement with you gives us first call on your services. Are you suggesting that you are going to raise your fee again?"

"No," I said modestly. "I think that three hundred dollars a day and expenses is adequate—until there's another rise in the cost of living. I was thinking more in terms of a bonus, based on the amount of money I save for you."

"We'll discuss that in the next board meeting," he said gravely. "We'll let you know in Reno. I want you to take a plane this afternoon so you'll be there and ready to go early tomorrow morning."

"I think we have a communication gap, Martin. I know, of course, it will have to be discussed with all the wheels, and I have a suggestion which should make it work out for everyone. It'll give you time to talk it over before everyone scatters for the usual three-hour luncheon, and enough time to write me a letter telling me the answer, which you will send to me at my apartment by messenger. In the meantime, I'll make a reservation on a plane leaving this afternoon. If the answer is yes, I'll be aboard the plane; if not, I'll have time to cancel the reservation."

"Damnit, Milo, this is a barefaced holdup," he said angrily.

"You've already been held up. You want me to save as much money for you as I can. Since it's a tough situation, I think it's only right that I should be rewarded with a percentage of what I save."

He stood up and walked across his office to stare out the window. "I suppose you have a figure in mind?"

"Yes," I admitted. "It just came to me. I believe you'll find it fair. Let's say one percent of what I save."

"What the hell is wrong with you, Milo?" he demanded. "One of these days you'll go too far."

"I'll save my bonus," I promised, "so I can afford the fare. Why don't you noodle it with the boys in the back room?"

"I'll tell them what you're asking," he said grimly, "and have my girl phone you the answer. Either way, you'd better be in Reno tomorrow morning." He turned to face me so I could see how serious he was.

I stood up and smiled. "You'd better take care of yourself, Martin. I'd hate to learn that anything happened to you right after our friendly talk." I turned and left the office, closing the door gently behind me.

His secretary looked up at me. "Well, that was quite a session you had with him. I have a couple of things here for you." She held out two envelopes, filled with papers, shaking her head as I took them. "I don't know how you do it."

"Do what?"

"Pry him loose from so much money. Especially when you're headed for Reno.

That's a good place to get a divorce from your money."

"Not me. I neither drink, chase women, nor gamble when I'm working for dear old Intercontinental. If you think this is bad, wait until you see what hits the fan when he comes out of that office."

"I shudder to think. But if he is coming, you'd better struggle along, love. If he sees you standing here with that lewd grin on your face, he won't know whether it's because of the money you're holding or me."

"If only it were you … ," I said, letting it trail off.

"Knock it off, buster. Run along and wave your ill-gotten money in the face of the first pretty wench you see."

"That I shall do, but it will do me no good. There would be muttering and grumbling if I took her to Reno with me. I shall wait impatiently to hear from you."

"Why?"

"Because I will. He'll tell you so himself. I'll see you around, honey."

I walked back down the corridor and into the reception room. Carmen looked up and gave me a smile as I went over to her desk.

"How'd you make out?" she asked.

"Like a thief," I said. "But I come bearing bad news."

"They didn't fire you."

"They're thinking it over," I said. "But I had intended to stop and bully you into having dinner with me. Unfortunately, I'll have to postpone it."

"You asked Mr. Raymond's secretary first and she said yes?"

"No. I have to get on a plane and go to Reno this afternoon. Want to come along?"

"I'd love to, but I don't think it's a good idea."

"Damn," I said. "I thought it was a good idea. It would give me a chance to walk into someplace with you and not find your roommate waiting there for us."

She laughed. "Kitty's a good girl."

"I wasn't doubting her morals a bit," I said indignantly. "But I think she's a little young to spend all of her life being a chaperone."

"I'll tell her you're concerned about her."

"You do that. Well, I'll see you when I get back. If I get back."

"What's that supposed to mean?" she asked.

"Well—it is a pretty dangerous assignment."

She laughed again. "Don't forget you have to catch a plane. I wouldn't want you to lose your job because of me. If anything does happen to you, I'll send flowers."

I glared at her. "You're all feeling, girl. What are you doing? Running for national office in the Women's Lib movement?" I left, but she was still laughing when I entered the elevator.

I took a taxi down to my apartment on Perry Street in the Village. There was no mail in the box, not even bills. I went upstairs. I dropped the papers on the kitchen table and put the money in my pocket. Then I called United Airlines and got a reservation on the four o'clock flight. I glanced at my watch and decided I had enough time, so I went downstairs and walked to the Blue Mill.

I had a martini at the bar and talked to Alcino for a few minutes, then went to a table and ordered lunch. When I had finished, I went back to the apartment. I packed a suitcase, putting my gun and holster in a special compartment. I tossed the papers on top of the clothes. I could read them later.

I splashed some brandy in a glass and sat down on the couch. I drank it slowly, then glanced at my watch again. There was still time, so I stretched out on the couch and went to sleep.

The ringing of the doorbell awakened me. I struggled across the room and opened the door. It was a messenger boy. I tipped him and took the envelope. As soon as he was gone, I opened it. The letter said that I was to receive one percent of any moneys I saved Intercontinental on a settlement of the insurance policy which had been issued to the Natural Gold Mine Corporation of Reno, Nevada.

The phone rang. I scooped up the receiver and said hello.

"Hello," she said. It was Raymond's secretary. "Did you get your letter? Mr. Raymond wanted me to call and make sure you received it and will be on the plane this afternoon."

"Yes on both counts. You did a beautiful job of typing."

"I always try," she said demurely. "You pulled off a pretty good con game yourself. You must have twisted somebody's arm."

"Not me. It was simple. They were so anxious to grab on to something that looked easy and it turned out it wasn't. They think they will be way ahead of the game if I manage to save them a few thousand dollars, and one percent won't mean much. I, on the other hand, think they have a tough problem but that I can save them the entire two million dollars. One percent of that is pretty good walking-around money and not to be sneezed at."

"I hear you loud and clear," she said. "When you know that you're going to save the entire amount, let me know. I think I might take my vacation then."

"Martin's taking it that badly?"

"I wouldn't go so far as to say that. All I know is that he had me call his club today and make a luncheon reservation—for one."

"The manhattans will cheer him up," I said. "I'll see you around."

"I'm sure you will. But it's the cashier you're going to drive to a nervous breakdown. Good luck." She hung up.

I picked up the papers in my suitcase and opened them. I thought I'd do a little homework. But the phone rang again. I lifted the receiver.

"Hello," I said.

"Mr. March?" a woman's voice asked.

"Speaking."

"There is an overseas call for you. Just a moment." I waited, wondering who was calling me. The operator cut in again. "Your party is on the line, Mr. March," she said.

"Thank you," I said. I waited, listening to the strange noises coming over the wire. Then she said hello. There could be no mistake about that voice. It belonged to Hsu Mei or, as she preferred, Mei Hsu, placing her given name first, in Western fashion. She lived in Hong Kong, and I had known her for a long time. I was more fond of her than I usually cared to admit.*

* Milo and Mei first met in *Jade for a Lady.*

"Hello, Mei," I said. "Where are you?"

"Home. In Hong Kong. Are you glad I called?"

"Very much. Is everything all right?"

"Everything is wonderful—now that I hear your voice. I am coming to America. Do you remember that you invited me?"

"Of course I do. When will you be here?"

"I have a reservation on a plane leaving Hong Kong at eight o'clock tomorrow evening. It arrives in Los Angeles on Tuesday at four in the morning. Then I have only to fly from Los Angeles to New York, and you will meet me and I will be there, yes?"

"Not exactly, darling. Instead, when you get to Los Angeles, you will take a plane to Reno, Nevada. I will meet you there, yes."

"Why Reno?"

"Because I'm leaving for Reno in a couple of hours. I have to do some work there. But while I'm working, you can go to the casinos and gamble and then we'll go out and play every night. Okay?"

"How near is Reno to Los Angeles?"

"Very near. Since you arrive in Los Angeles at four in the morning, your biggest problem is what time you can get a plane out. As soon as you're through customs, find out about a flight to Reno and call me at the Pony Express Hotel, and then I'll meet you at the airport. We can have breakfast together."

"That sounds wonderful, Milo. Where will I be staying in Reno?"

"With me—if you can stand it. When I check into the hotel,

I will tell them that my wife will be arriving Tuesday morning. And that's all there will be to it."

"Sounds lovely. I've never been on a honeymoon before."

"There's all sorts of good things in America."

She laughed. "I'll see you Tuesday morning, darling. Goodbye for now." There was a click as she hung up.

I sat for a minute, thinking about her. It was going to be nice to see her again.

I picked up the phone and called my answering service. I told them I would be out of town for an indefinite period and would call them as soon as I got back. I got undressed and took a shower. I put on a fresh suit and closed my suitcase.

Downstairs I hailed a cab and told the driver to take me to Kennedy Airport. I lit a cigarette and leaned back, thinking about Mei. I hadn't seen her since I'd stopped off in Hong Kong on my way to South Africa.*

The driver made good time to the terminal. I went in and found the United counter. I picked up my ticket and my seat number, and checked my suitcase for the flight.

There was still some time until the plane could be boarded, so I went into a bar and ordered a dry martini. When it came I sipped it and waited for an announcement that it was time to board the plane.

"Paging Mr. March," a voice said from a loudspeaker. "Will Mr. Milo March please come to the United Airlines counter." I finished my drink and strolled out of the bar. I walked up to the airlines counter. There was a man leaning on it. As I stepped up to the counter, a girl hurried toward me.

---

* See *Green Grow the Graves* by M.E. Chaber.

"May I help you, sir?" she asked.

"My name is Milo March. You just paged me."

She glanced to one side, and I was aware that the man had moved down next to me.

"Is your name Milo March?" he asked.

"I just said it was. Did you have me paged?"

"Yes. I want to talk to you."

"Why?"

"I'll tell you if you'll just step across to the door over there. Then we can talk alone."

"My mother always told me not to go into rooms with a strange man," I said.

"Besides, you smell like fuzz."

He reached into his coat and brought out a slim ID case and flipped it open. I looked at it. "You're fuzz," I said. "You're Federal fuzz. The worst kind. Does Washington know you're out harassing the citizens?"

"Through the door," he said. The folder was back in his pocket, but his hand stayed near it.

I shrugged and walked ahead of him through the door.

TWO

There was another man in the room. His gaze went to the man behind me, then flicked to me and stayed. There was also a long table and on it a suitcase that looked familiar. It was mine.

"This is March," the man behind me said. "Watch him while I check him out."

A second later, I felt the hands of the first man frisking me all the way down to my ankles. Then he stood up and moved around in front of me. "You're Milo March," he said flatly.

"That's what I told you," I said. "Do you have a name, or does everybody just call you baby?"

He didn't like that. "Just stick to answering questions. Where were you headed?"

"Reno, Nevada."

"Why?"

"Business trip."

"Doing what?"

"That's my business," I said gently.

"We can make it our business."

I shook my head. "You wouldn't like it. It involves being accosted by strange fuzz who can't wait until they can get their hands on you to pat you. Know what I mean, baby?"

"You'd better know what *we* mean," he said grimly. He didn't seem to like me. I wondered why.

"How can I, when you don't tell me what this is all about? What do you want? Why am I here? What is that suitcase doing here?"

"You admit that it belongs to you?"

"No, I don't," I said. "It looks like mine, but I can't be sure from here. If it is mine, I want to know why it's here instead of being loaded on the plane."

"Let's look at it," he said. The three of us walked over to it. "Well?"

"It's mine. Now you answer my question."

"As you must know, all luggage going into planes is checked these days. Our instruments indicate that there's a piece of metal in there. A fairly large piece of metal. What is it?"

I laughed. "Why didn't you ask right away? It's a gun and some shells."

"Why are you taking a gun aboard the plane to Reno?"

"Because it's part of my business. I work as an investigator for a large insurance company, and I'm going to Reno to investigate a possible case of fraud against them. The gun is one of the tools of my trade."

"Open the suitcase and show us."

"Okay." I reached to the suitcase and opened it. I lifted the clothes and put my hand down inside and opened the secret compartment. Then, showing my hands were empty, I stepped slowly back two paces. "Look for yourselves."

The two men looked at each other for a second, then the first one stepped forward. He put his hand beside the clothes and carefully felt around. He pulled out the gun and looked at it. "Planning on using this?" he asked.

"If I have to."

"Anybody ever tell you that it's against the law?"

"A few have," I said. "If you want to charge me with illegal possession of a gun, try it on for size. I carried the gun from my apartment here to Kennedy Airport, where I turned it over to a common carrier to transport it to Reno, Nevada, where I will once more carry it. I have a license to carry that gun here and also in Nevada. You boys have a file on me with all the information on various licenses I carry and the serial number of the gun."

"I thought your name was familiar," the second agent said. "You're the guy who messed up our case when that congressman was killed in Cleveland."*

"I messed it up so badly that I solved it and got the man you were looking for. I'd better add one thing for your information. If you arrest me for having that gun or cause me to miss this flight for any reason connected with you two, you'd better be prepared for some heat."

"Are you threatening us?"

"Me? I don't have any heat. But I work for the Intercontinental Insurance Company, Incorporated, and they do. In the case that you mentioned, you may also remember that the company paid off on the congressman's insurance and paid all costs for tracking down the man you couldn't find and for my getting him and turning him over to you in Paris. I also found a witness who gave information concerning the men who were behind the scheme. And the company takes a dim view of anyone hampering the pursuit of my duties for them."

---

* See *Green Grow the Graves.*

The first agent glanced at his watch. "If you're going to make that plane, you'd better start moving."

"Thanks," I said dryly. "Since you boys took possession of my suitcase, I expect you to see that it is put aboard in the hold before we take off. Since I wouldn't want the scanner to also locate the gun on my person, I think you'd better replace it in the suitcase before you close it."

I handed the gun to the agent, who took it, muttering something beneath his breath. I didn't hear it because I was heading for the door as fast as I could. I made it just seconds before they closed the gate. I entered the plane and found my seat. There was still a short delay before the plane took off, and I smiled to myself.

Finally we were in the air. The plane climbed steeply until, below, New York City looked like a bunch of fat old ladies and men sleeping off a wine blast. When the smoking sign went on, I lit a cigarette and half listened as the pilot told us over the loudspeaker where we were going, when we'd get there, the speed we'd be traveling, and the altitude. Then things began to brighten up. A stewardess came down the aisle taking orders for drinks, soft or otherwise. I ordered a double dry martini. She gave me a quick glance and apparently decided I knew what I was doing.

I leaned back against the seat and waited. The first-class section had a good many empty seats, including the one next to me.

My stewardess was augmented by another when the serving started. They moved speedily, but I noticed that I was going to be the last one to be served. That could mean one of three things. She didn't like me, she did like me, or she was just curious. I made a silent bet on the last.

I pulled down the serving table as she reached me. She put the cocktail glass and two tiny bottles, each holding enough for one martini. I thanked her and opened one bottle, pouring it into the glass.

"Going to Reno?" she asked when I had taken the first sip.

"Yes."

"Live there?"

I shook my head. "New York."

She smiled. "Going there to try your luck?"

"Maybe, but not in the way you mean. I might like a fling once in a while, but I prefer to stick to my two main vices. Drinking and women."

This time she laughed. "I had that already figured. But not necessarily in that order?"

"Not necessarily in that order," I admitted, returning her smile. "You stay over in Reno?"

"No. I go on to San Francisco. Do you go to Reno often?"

"Once in a while. Then sometimes to Los Angeles—or San Francisco. And sometimes to South America or Europe."

"You must have an interesting job."

"Not so interesting," I said, "but it keeps me in enough money to afford my vices."

She leaned against the back of the seat next to me and looked down curiously.

This, I told myself, would reveal whether I had won my bet or not.

"You almost missed the plane," she said. So that was it.

She was curious.

"It was close," I admitted, "but I made it, thanks to pure thoughts and clean living."

"I noticed that we had to hold the plane up while a final piece of luggage was brought out. Was that yours, too?"

"It was."

"That's what I thought," she said with satisfaction. "Did they think that you were going to hijack the plane?"

"A couple of gentlemen did have some such idea, but I gather that they dismissed the thought."

"Did you intend to hijack the plane?"

I finished the drink in my glass, took the top off the second bottle, and poured the contents into the glass. I lifted it and stared at her over the rim.

"Didn't anyone ever tell you that little girls who ask too many questions may get in trouble?"

"They told me a lot of things," she said. "The only way to find out whether they were telling the truth or not was to ask a lot of questions. Did you?"

"Did I what?"

"Plan to hijack the plane?" She sounded eager.

"It never entered my mind," I admitted. "I hadn't lost a plane and I didn't have any burning desire to possess one. Besides, it's not the Cuban season just now.* However, just to make you happy, I'll brood about the possibility for a while."

---

* Between 1968 and 1972, more than 130 U.S. airplanes were hijacked; Cuba was the top hijacking destination during this period. In November 1972 three armed men hijacked a Southern Airlines flight from Birmingham, Alabama, forcing it to land in Havana under threat of crashing the plane into a nuclear reactor. It was after this incident that U.S. passengers were required to undergo a physical screening, passing through metal detectors and having their luggage searched.

Her curiosity satisfied for the time, she smiled happily and hurried off. I finished my martini, put the seat in a reclining position, and went to sleep. It's the best way to fly.

I was awakened when the plane came down at O'Hare Airport in Chicago. They were announcing that we'd be there only fifteen minutes but that we could get out if we wanted to. I didn't and went back to sleep. This time the motors awakened me as we taxied across the field.

As soon as we were high enough, I lit a cigarette and pushed the button for the stewardess. She came down the aisle, smiling as if we were old friends.

"Another double martini?" she asked. She was better than a lot of old friends.

"I thought you'd never ask," I told her. "I shall nominate you for the Gem of the Airways award."

She trotted off and soon returned with the two little bottles and the glass. I busied myself with one of the bottles.

"Do you mind if I ask you another question?" she asked.

"You just did," I pointed out, "but I presume that is not the one you meant. You'll do it anyway, so go ahead."

"What made the officers decide to search you back in New York?"

"That's easy. They were from the FBI and they're still looking for Jack the Ripper. I convinced them by showing them my birth certificate. It proved I was too young."

"No, really. You must have had some metal in your luggage. What was it?"

"A gun."

"Why?"

"Why a gun? Well, if someone broke into my luggage while I was asleep, I could still protect myself."

"But if your gun—" She broke off. "You're kidding me!"

"I thought you'd never guess." I took a drink and looked at her. "You ever been on a plane that was hijacked?"

"No."

"So, that's your problem. Did you ever have any dreams about hijacking a plane yourself?"

"Of course not!"

"Then I have one suggestion for you. The FBI has finally decided they will let a few female agents into their sacred circle. Why don't you apply? If nothing else, when you started asking questions, the meanest criminal would cower. I would give you a recommendation, but I'm not sure that would be any help. Do you live in San Francisco?"

"Yes."

"I'll make a deal with you. I'm going to finish my drink and go back to sleep. When it's time for dinner, bring a double martini and wake me up. Also bring a piece of paper on which you've written your name, address, and phone number, and the next time I'm in San Francisco I'll call you up. Maybe we'll hijack a cab, make the cab company fork over a couple hundred grand, and take a wild ride down to Mexico."

"You're just making fun of me—but all right." She turned and was gone.

I sipped my drink and stared out the window. There was nothing to see except a few wispy clouds. I had seen a cloud before, so I finished the second martini and leaned back. It took me only a few minutes to fall asleep.

I felt someone shaking my shoulder and I opened my eyes. It was the stewardess with my martini. "We're going to start serving dinner soon," she said. She placed the glass and bottles on the shelf in front of me and then added a folded piece of paper next to them. "We have—"

"You don't have to run through the whole inventory for me," I said gently. "I'll have a rare steak and whatever you're serving to go with it." I picked up the paper and unfolded it. It was her name, address, and phone number. Or, at least, somebody's. I put it in my inside coat pocket. "I will carry it next to my heart. My name is—"

"I know your name," she interrupted. "It's Milo March."

"How do you know that? Do I talk in my sleep?"

She shook her head. "I had one of the boys radio back to New York and find out."

"Well, that's one way." I opened one of the bottles and poured it into the glass.

"Do you always drink that much?" she asked.

"No, sometimes I drink more."

"That's terrible."

"What's terrible about it? How far are we from Reno now?"

"Two or two and a half hours. Why?"

"That's the trouble with using a cloud as a landmark. It's moving all the time. The reason for asking the time is this. We're almost five hours out of New York City. It's a medical fact that a man of my size can drink an ounce of liquor an hour and never feel it. So I will have had six ounces and a dinner in seven hours. That is, I'll have the six ounces if you run along and do your kitchen work."

She went on her way, but I could tell she was thinking it over and knew she'd be asking a lot of people about the ounce-an-hour theory before the end of the following day. I grinned to myself and concentrated on the gin and vermouth in front of me.

The dinner arrived at just about the right time. I finished the martini and gave the same loving care to the steak. It was just right. I polished off the entire meal and then had a glass of milk.* The stewardess came to remove the dishes and told me we'd be in Reno within an hour. I lit a cigarette and for the first time began looking out the window. We were low enough so that I could see the sides of mountains and occasionally a stream cutting its way between the towering earth and rocks on either side. Far below, there was a highway stretching like a narrow ribbon across the landscape. And, occasionally, small roads leading up into hills, looking like wavering pencil marks.

It was still light when the No Smoking and seat belt sign flashed in front of us. I turned my watch back three hours as we glided down to the runway.

I waited until there were only a few people left in the plane, then got up and walked toward the exit. The stewardesses were waiting there to say good-bye to all of us. I winked at the one who had served me.

It took only a few minutes to reclaim my baggage and get a cab. The driver put my suitcase in the back and I told him to take me to the Pony Express Hotel.

---

* With this meal high in protein and fat, Milo may be slowing down the rate of alcohol absorption in his gut.

It was a short drive to the hotel. A bellman saw the cab arrive and was outside waiting before I got out. The driver lifted my bag out of the rear. I paid him and followed the bellman into the hotel lobby and up to the desk. I told him to wait and filled out the card the clerk put in front of him. He turned it around and looked at it.

"I thought you had been here before," he said. "Glad to have you with us again, Mr. March. A single?"

"No," I said. "I want a double. I'm here on business and not sure how long I will remain, but my wife is joining me in a few days. She can while the time away at the tables while I'm out working. She'll like that."

"Fine, Mr. March." He reached up behind him and pulled a key from the mailbox. I turned to the bellman and gave him a dollar. "I'm in four thirty-six," I told him. "Put my bag in the room. I'm going to stroll around for a few minutes."

"Yes, sir," he said, and was gone.

I walked through the lobby and entered the casino. Most of the tables were busy. I wasn't hung up on gambling, but I decided to give something a little play. I went to the cashier and got fifty silver dollars. I had to put some of them in my coat pocket. Carrying the rest, I walked over to the dollar slot machine and fed one into it.

It got to be a habit. I lost thirty dollars before I hit anything. Then I kept hitting a few and losing a few more. Finally I was down to two dollars. It was the hour of truth. I put one in and hit. I put the second one in and hit again. I took a dollar out of the trough and dropped it in, thinking I'd be friendly to the management. It hit once more. I said to hell with the management, gathered up my dollars, and staggered over to the cashier's cage.

I got sixty-nine dollars from the girl, all in folding money. I was nineteen dollars ahead. It spoiled the fun I would have gotten putting the fifty dollars on the expense account.

I went outside and walked slowly down the street. It was dark by this time. The air was cool and dry. Ahead of me I saw an Eagle Thrifty store still open and decided to go in there.

When I came out of the store, I was carrying a bottle of gin and a container of orange juice in a paper bag. The evening newspaper was under my arm. I walked back to the hotel and went straight up to my room. After taking off my jacket and hanging it up, I phoned room service and ordered a bucket of ice.

When it arrived I tipped the waiter at the door and carried it across the room to a table next to the window. I picked up a glass from the bathroom and got the papers from my jacket and took them back to the table. Then I made a gin and orange juice and lit a cigarette.

Finally I picked up the Intercontinental papers and spread them on the table. I decided I might as well do my homework.

The first thing I saw was the name of a company. The Natural Gold Mine Corporation. There was an address in Reno.

Next were the names of the three officers. Dino Mancetti, Jerry Lake, and Nick Lancer. They also had Reno addresses. I was about to go on when something made me go back to look at the names again.

Dino Mancetti. There was something familiar about that name. I took another long pull on the glass and lit a fresh cigarette. The cigarette had almost burned down to my fingers when I remembered.

I had been in Reno a few years earlier to get some information about a man I was trying to find. That was when I heard the name. Dino Mancetti was a fairly small man in the Syndicate.

At that time, I seemed to remember, he was involved in a fairly prosperous semi-legal business. Now he was one of the owners of a gold mine.

THREE

That brought up some interesting possibilities. I couldn't see anyone in the Syndicate actually digging for gold. It had to be a front for something else. But I couldn't imagine its being a front for anything except gold. That was pretty silly.

The other two names meant nothing to me. I could probably find out the next morning. I already doubted they could be solid citizens. It made me feel that the whole insurance policy was a way of getting home free with two million dollars. There might be some gold in the mine, so the two million would be a bonus.

I looked over the rest of the information. Some of it had already been given to me by Martin Raymond. Not much. He had stressed the amount of money they were stealing from the company, and he had mentioned the assayer, a Manfred Smith. Now I had the names of the three men and the name of the mine. It was the Natural Gold Mine Corporation. There were two ways to read the name. One was that it meant it was a mine with a natural vein of gold running through it. The second was more interesting. In a dice game when you throw a seven or eleven on the first throw, it's called a natural.

I made another drink and looked at the rest of the paper. There wasn't much in it. The mine had been discovered a long time ago by an old prospector. He'd set up the All Mine

Gold Company and had worked it himself for a number of years. Then apparently the old man had exhausted the one vein of gold and had just walked off and left it. That had been so far back that nobody remembered where the mine had been and who, if anyone, had last owned it.

Obviously everyone knew who owned it now, as well as where it was. There was only one real question. Why, and how, was it suddenly producing gold after so many dry years? I had to find the answer to that question and to another one. Why was a member of the Syndicate suddenly in the mining business?

The answer wasn't in the rest of the information that Intercontinental had given me. I folded the papers and slipped them into my shirt pocket. I picked up my drink, walked over and turned on the television, then crossed to one of the two beds and sat down. I lit a cigarette and picked up the newspaper I'd bought.

The show on the screen wasn't anything special, but I left it on and opened the paper. Several minutes later I tossed it to one side. There was only one thing in it that interested me. It was about Dino Mancetti. He was offering to buy some property and turn it into a ball diamond for Little Leaguers. A group of citizens were opposed to it. There wasn't anything in it for me.

Finally I decided I was hungry. I called room service and ordered a club sandwich and a glass of milk. I made myself another drink and watched television until the waiter arrived. I signed the tab and added a tip for him. A better show had come on the screen, and I settled down to watch it. My timing was good. I finished my sandwich just as the show ended. I turned off the set, drank my milk, and went to bed.

It was early when I awakened the next morning. I ordered some breakfast from room service and went into the bathroom for a quick shower and a shave. When the knock came on the door, I was ready. I let the waiter in and he set the tray on the table by the window. He took a paper from beneath his arm and placed it beside the tray.

"The morning paper?" I asked. "How much is it?"

"It's on the house," he said, and started to add up the bill. I knew what he meant. He expected the tip to add to a fund to build him a house. I signed for it and added his tip. I saw him take a quick glance at it, and he was smiling as he left. He probably thought that if I stayed long enough, he could enlarge the house by another room.

I had a small drink and tackled the breakfast. It was good, and I finished all of it, including the milk. I took the gun and holster from my bag and buckled it on. Then I slipped on my coat and left. It was a workday.

Downstairs, I stopped at the desk and had the girl call the Deluxe Cab Company and ask for Big Jack. I sat down on a couch near the desk and waited.

It didn't take long. I was up and out through the door by the time he got out of the cab. He wasn't called Big Jack for nothing. He was at least six feet seven inches, and they hadn't cheated on the chassis either.

"Hello, Milo," he said as he saw me. "When did you get in?"

"Last night. On the eight o'clock plane."

"Good trip?"

"The same as always. You'd think they'd change the scenery once in a while."

He was polite. He laughed. "Here on business?"

"Yeah."

"I noticed the piece," he said. "Where do you want to go?"

"I'm not sure. I noticed on the way to the hotel last night that the Jug is now a place where the girls hang out. A topless joint. Where's the old action at?"

"A couple of places. Your best bet is probably the Tun. There's a couple of bartenders there you'll know."

"Let's try it, then. Who thought of calling it the Tun? That used to be a cask that was used for wine. If that gives any indication of how they pour, I think I'll order a martini and see what I get."

He laughed. "They'll short-pour you no matter what you order."

"I suppose they will." I sighed. "What's Dino doing these days when he's not building a baseball diamond? I saw the story in the paper last night."

"That's Dino. Anything to get publicity. He's still doing all right with the Palomino Mare. I hear there's a great bunch of girls working there now. I took two dudes out last night, and they raved all the way back."

"How's he doing in the gold-mining business?"

"You heard about that, huh? I don't get what that scam is—unless it's just another way of getting his name in the paper. That mine's been empty for years. You sound interested."

"I am. When he bought the mine, he insured it against the vein of gold running out. Now he's trying to collect—two million dollars."

He whistled. "That's a lot of gold. Think they'll collect?"

"Over my dead body. At least, that's the way the insurance company sees it. Do you know a guy named Manfred Smith? He's supposed to be a gold assayer."

"I know him," Jack said. "He has an office with a sign saying he's a lawyer and a gold assayer. I understand that he has two diplomas on the wall inside. One from a law school and one from a mining school."

"Does he make a living?"

"He must. He has a nice house in the northwest of town and drives a Lincoln."

"How does he make his money? He charged five hundred dollars for his report on the mine, but he'd have to make a lot of reports to earn that kind of money."

"He's a scam artist," Jack said, "but from what I've heard, the kind who stays right at the edge of the dividing line. So he's considered on the right side of the law. I hear that he spends a lot of time at the courthouse looking at documents that have been filed and also has a large law library. Whenever some lawyer, especially a corporation lawyer, pulls a blooper, he knows it right away. Then he sits back and waits."

"For what?"

"One of the two parties begins to think that there is something wrong with the agreement he's made, but before his lawyers can find it, Smith gets in touch with the one he knows will win and sells his knowledge and himself. Or he waits until he knows the statute of limitations may decide it, then he also goes to the one he knows will be the winner."

"Clever," I said, "but I wouldn't think there'd be too many cases like that."

"Not many," Jack said, "but apparently enough. Smith had to testify once about how much money he had made the year before. It was a hundred thousand dollars. A man could live all right if he had one case like that every two years."

"True," I admitted. "What about the two men who are in the gold mine with Dino?"

"They're both scam artists, too. I hear they recently took over a good business in stolen TV and radio sets out of Reno. Sold in San Francisco. And I've also heard that they have a little drug business in San Francisco and sometimes work as hired guns, but only for one outfit."

"That figures. Thanks, Jack."

"For what? You'll have to prove it. You can't convict any of them on what anyone has heard."

"I'm sorry you reminded me of that," I said dryly. "I guess I have to fall back on the March Method."

"Which is?"

"Start pushing people and wait to see who pushes back."

Jack swung the cab over to the curb in front of a bar. The sign in front of it announced the Tun. "I think," he said, "I may take a vacation for a couple of weeks. It always upsets me when I see a good cab with bullet holes in it."

I laughed. "I wouldn't do that to a good taxi. I'm going to rent a car sometime today." I paid him and got out.

Inside, it looked like any other bar. There were six men and two girls seated down the bar. I remembered the faces of some of them. I took a stool at the end of the bar where I could see everyone. The bartender strolled up to me. He had worked at the Jug when I'd last been there—before it went topless.

"Hello, Don," I said as he drew near.

He took a closer look at me. "Hello, Milo," he said. "I haven't seen you in a couple of years."

"About that," I admitted. "I got in last night. I learned from Big Jack this morning that there was no point in going to the old joints unless I just wanted to keep abreast of the times."

"That's about it," he said, laughing. "Here on business?"

"That's what the company thinks. In the meantime, I'll have a gin and grapefruit on the rocks. Go light on the grapefruit. I don't want to overdo this vitamin C bit."

He made the drink and put it in front of me. I put money on the bar. "Have one yourself."

"That's the first good thing I've heard this morning," he said. He got a bottle of beer and came back up to where I sat.

"How are things with you?" I asked.

"The same as always. What are you doing here? You know we don't have any crime in Reno."

"I've noticed," I said dryly. "I'm out here to dig up some information about gold mines."

His eyebrows went up about a half inch. "Gold mines? You thinking about buying one?"

"Not unless they're running a white sale. I just want to find out about some of the old mines around here. Nothing else to do."

"You and Dino Mancetti."

"Yeah. What's he going to do with it? Paper the walls of the Palomino Mare with gold leaf?"

"I don't know. Maybe he just wants the publicity. Although I hear he's taken some gold out of it." The door opened and two old men came in. "Here comes your chance," he said, lowering his voice. "They know all about the old mines."

"Buy them drinks," I said quickly. "And bring me another one."

He nodded and moved over to where they were sitting down. I took a quick look at them. They were both probably in their early sixties. They wore faded Levi's, flannel shirts, and cowboy hats.

Don took their orders and went to make the three drinks. He stopped in front of them as he came back. "This gentleman," he said, pointing to me, "wants you to drink with him. Do you want yours here, or do you want to join him?"

They looked at me. "Might as well," one of them said. They came over and sat on the stools next to me. Don was already there with the drinks. He placed them on the bar and moved away with my money.

"Thank you, mister," the one said.

"Cheers," I said. "My name is Milo March."

"Glad to meet you," the same man said. "I'm Homer Ambrose Fenner. This here is Johnny Murphy. Stranger in town?"

"Pretty much so. I've been here several times, but I live in New York City."

"Been there once," Fenner said. "Didn't like it. You here for a little fling at the tables, or on business?"

"Business. I'm trying to dig up some stories on gold mines."

They both looked at me with new interest. "Newspaper fellow?"

"Sort of," I said casually. "You fellows been around here long?"

"All our lives. I got a little old mine not far from here. Necktie's been digging or panning most of his life."

"Necktie?" I said. "That's an unusual name."

"Reckon it is," Murphy said. "When I was a little shaver, my pappy always said I was born to be hanged. When I got older, the fellows started calling me Necktie."

"Well," I said, "it looks as if you outlived the prediction."

"Ain't yet," he said, shaking his head. "And I don't remember pappy ever calling a prediction that didn't come true. But I've been ready for it for sixty years."

"He'll still be saying the same thing twenty years from now," Fenner said. "He's too ornery to die young. What kind of mines you interested in?"

"Old ones."

"I got an old one. Called the Lucky Goddess Mine. Won it in a poker game when I was still a young fellow."

"Has it been, Mr. Fenner?"

"Most people call me Ambrose," he said. "My father wanted me named after Ambrose Bierce.* ... Has it been what?"

"Has the Lucky Goddess been lucky for you?"

He thought about it for a minute. "Well, she has and she hasn't. Just like a woman. I got her about thirty years ago. I

---

* Ambrose Bierce was known for his satirical writings and his supernatural horror fiction. His celebrated lexicon, *The Devil's Dictionary*, now seems outdated and offensive, but often still witty and on the mark. Examples: *Dog*. A kind of additional or subsidiary Deity designed to catch the overflow and surplus of the world's worship. *Kill*. To create a vacancy without nominating a successor. *Selfish*. Devoid of consideration for the selfishness of others. *Telephone*. An invention of the devil which abrogates some of the advantages of making a disagreeable person keep his distance.

used to work it very hard but didn't strike it rich. I guess it had been pretty well worked out. Now I only work it two or three days and maybe get as high as two ounces of gold a week. Ain't much, but it gives me as much money as I need."

"You have any family, Ambrose?"

"Neither hen nor chick. So I get along all right. Me and Necktie, here, we dig out enough to keep us alive."

"Are you two partners?"

"In a way, I reckon, you could say that. The mine's in my name, but Necktie's been my friend for thirty years and he works right alongside of me. We both get enough, and it gives me somebody to talk to. That counts for something when you're getting older."

"It counts for a lot," I said. I noticed that their glasses were empty, and I motioned to Don. "Maybe you'll still hit it. There might be a bigger vein that you haven't found yet."

"That's what I keep telling him," Necktie said, "but the old fool won't listen to me. Thinks he knows it all."

"You picked out a dozen big rocks," Ambrose answered, "and never found a speck of gold. If there'd been a bigger vein, I'd of found it years ago. No, the main vein just missed me, I reckon."

"What about that fellow next to you?" Necktie demanded. "He's got a vein that doesn't go the same way as mine, that's all."

"There's a mine I wonder if you know anything about," I put in. "It's called the Natural Gold Mine."

They looked at each other, then turned back to look at me again. "How come you're interested in that one?" Ambrose asked. He didn't sound quite as friendly as before.

"A lot of reasons," I said casually. "I don't know him personally, but I do know the name and the reputation of one of the three men who own it. I'm curious about why he's in the mining business."

"A lot of people wonder about that," Ambrose said. "You mean Dino, don't you?"

I nodded.

"Well, I can tell you one thing," he said. "Dino never went into anything unless he was sure there was money in it."

"How come somebody didn't take over the mine before this?"

"I don't rightly know. Over the years, a bunch of smart men have gone through that mine with a toothbrush, but never found a speck of gold."

"Until an assayer named Manfred Smith stated that there was a rich vein in it."

"Manny Smith wouldn't know gold if it was right in one of his teeth."

"But he is an assayer, isn't he?" I asked.

"He's got a paper that says he is."

"But you don't think he's a very good one. Is that it?"

"I reckon that's about it," he said. "Maybe I ain't very fair about it. The truth is that I never did cotton to the fellow. Never had much to do with him until a few years ago I went up and was grubbing around in my mine when I hit some traces of gold. I decided I'd better get an assayer to look it over. I didn't have much money, and the asking price was too steep for me. Smith wasn't doing so good then, and I heard he'd do it cheap and even wait for his money if he thought the gold was there. I went to see him and told him what I wanted."

"He took the job right then?"

"Not right off. Said he'd meet me up at the mine the next day. He did and I showed him what I'd found. He got interested then. Said he'd look at it a little closer and he'd only charge me two hundred dollars, and I could pay him out of the gold I dug out."

"That was pretty fair," I said. "Wasn't it?"

"No quarrel with that," he said. "He had the report for me in about a week. He said that there was some gold there, but not very much. He thought I could maybe get a few hundred dollars and then there wouldn't be no more gold. That's when I got the idea he was a little crooked."

"Why?"

"Well, like I said, that was several years ago. It's been worked steadily since then."

"By you?"

"First by me and then by me and Necktie. The first two weeks I worked pretty hard and paid him off. Since then the mine's been worked kind of easy-like. We just took what was needed for the two of us. Man don't need a lot of money to be happy."

"But why did you think he was a crook?" I asked.

"Well, it seemed likely. Maybe there was two veins in there. One of them a small one and one a big one. Maybe the one we been working is the small one and he never told me about it, figuring that later, when I thought it was about finished, he'd send along a guy to offer me a price for the mine, figuring I was a sucker and would sell it."

"That's what I've been tellin' you," Necktie said. "I bet he's the one that put Dino up to buying the mine right next to you and the two of them is partners. Old slippery Smith figured the big vein runs through the other mine, and he then put up the dough for Dino to take it over. It's your gold they been carrying out of there."

"Maybe," Ambrose said, "but I don't think there's any other vein running through both mines. It don't make sense."

"It makes sense to me. You're just too danged stubborn to see it."

I decided to stop it before it became a full-blown argument. "Ambrose," I said, "I'd like to see your mine."

"Don't see no harm in that," he said. "When?"

"Anytime that's good for you."

"How about this afternoon?" he asked. "Me and Necktie ain't got nothin' to do except to sit around soaking up this booze."

"How do you usually get to it?"

"Walk. It might be a far piece for you, for it's a brisk walk. Don't reckon you do much of that where you come from."

"Not much," I admitted. "Can't we get to it by car? I was going to rent one this afternoon anyway."

"Yeah. We can get there by car, but you make sure it's one with a four-wheel drive. That ain't no big highway running up there."

"Okay. What time do I pick you up and where?"

Ambrose took an old watch out of his pocket and squinted at it. "Reckon it's about time for me and Necktie to stop in and see Jed at his bar. It's right down the street. Jed's Bar. You can't miss it. Maybe about three o'clock."

"I'll be there."

"Want to tell you one thing," Necktie said. "Them fellows'll be at the mine next to us. There every day. One of them stands out in the front with a big sawed-off shotgun. Looks mean enough to use it, too."

"I'll worry about him after we get there. See you at Jed's."

They nodded and both of them shook hands with me. Then they plodded out of the bar.

Don came up to me. "Want another drink?" he asked.

"I guess I can stand another one."

He took my glass and mixed another one. He put it in front of me and pushed my money back to me. "What was that all about?" he asked.

"They told me about their mine, and they're going to take me up to see it this afternoon."

"You're going to walk up Mount Peavine? Sounds like you've blown a fuse."

"You should know better than that, Don. There are only two times I will walk, and only then if there's no other way. One is to get a drink and the other to reach a beautiful woman. Not necessarily in that order."

"Do you know that you can't drive the average car up there? Especially a Cadillac or a Rolls, which you seem to prefer."

I finished my drink and shook my head as he reached for the glass. "You can't rent a Rolls around here," I told him. "But I'm going to rent a car. One with a four-wheel drive. In fact, I'm going now." I stood up.

"Okay. Don't pick up any wooden gold."

"If I do, I'll give it all to you. See you later." I left the bar and walked several blocks to a car-rental agency which I had used before when I was in Reno. A brisk young man came up to greet me.

"May I help you, sir?"

"You may try," I said. "I want to rent two cars."

"Two cars? That's a bit unusual, isn't it?"

"That depends. All of my wants are unusual. I want an LTD four-door and I want something with a four-wheel drive which will carry three people. I've rented from you before."

"Do you have a credit card?"

I took out my ID case and flipped it open. "You're in luck. You can take your choice. Either one of those."

"They're both quite all right, sir." His voice sounded more relaxed and friendly. "Do you mind, sir, if I ask why two such different cars?"

"I mind, but I'll tell you so you won't sulk all afternoon. I'm here on business. Part of that will take me out of the city, sometimes up in the hills, where a normal pleasure car will not function so well. Then my wife is arriving in a few days, and we will use the other for more pleasureful ventures. I trust that will satisfy all the requirements?"

"Yes, sir." He flushed a little but then he busied himself taking down all of the information about me. Where I worked, where I lived in New York, where I was staying in Reno, and other little things like that. Finally, his bookkeeping compulsions under control, he looked up. "When do you want the cars, sir?"

"Today. In fact, right now."

"You can have the LTD right now, but it'll be about an hour

before we can give you the four-wheel drive. It hasn't been out in some time and we'll want to check it."

"Okay. I'll take the LTD, and you can deliver the other at my hotel in an hour. I'll be there."

He nodded and called over another young man and told him to service the LTD and bring it around to the front. I signed all the papers, and by the time I was through, the car was out front. I got in and drove it off.

I made one stop and bought some clothes that would be more proper for the mountains. I included a loose-fitting jacket that wouldn't reveal my gun. I drove back to the hotel, parked the car, and went up to my room. I quickly changed into the new clothes and took a glance at myself in the mirror. I thought I looked rather like a city slicker about to embark on a Nevada safari.

Downstairs, I put four half-dollars in a slot machine to no avail and went on into the bar. I sipped my martini and waited for a delivery.

Finally, my name was called over a loudspeaker, and I went out and found the young man who was waiting. He took me out to the jeep, and I told him where to park it. After he had done so, we both got into the LTD, and I drove him back to the car rental place. He didn't say a word on the drive, so I guessed he'd been briefed about the crazy man who wanted two cars at the same time.

Then I went back to the hotel, parked the LTD, and got the jeep. I was glad to notice that it contained a two-way radio set. I'd forgotten to ask about one.

I parked downtown and went to the Waldorf. I sat at the bar

and had a couple of martinis while I shot the breeze with Joe. He thought the way I was dressed was pretty funny.

"If anybody sees you up in the mountain, he'll think that you're a revenuer and shoot you," he said.

"That doesn't bother me," I said, "and I've already figured out what to do if I run across a rattlesnake."

"What's that?"

"Faint."

"That shouldn't worry you," he said. "With all the snake-bite remedy you've stored up in you,* the snake won't do you any harm at all, but the snake will die of acute alcoholism."

"I didn't win the Drinker's Merit Badge for nothing," I said with dignity and went back to the dining room. I had a good, leisurely lunch and walked back to the jeep.

I made one stop on the way to Jed's Bar. I bought a quart of bourbon, three glasses, and some dry ice. I packed the ice around the bottle, put the whole thing in a bag, and drove on to the bar. I parked in front of it and went inside.

The two old men were there, still working on bourbon and looking none the worse for it.

"See you made it all right," Ambrose said. "Have a drink for the road? You might need it."

"Don't mind if I do," I said. I took one look at the bartender and decided not to risk a mixed drink. I ordered bourbon on the rocks.

A half hour later we were on our way. We went out West

---

* In the past, consuming alcohol *after* receiving a venomous snakebite (not in advance of a possible bite) was believed to be helpful, especially in emergency situations in remote areas. But today's medical authorities advise against drinking alcohol after a snakebite.

Seventh Street. After several miles the street narrowed but was still a solid road. I was grateful for that and the fact that there wasn't much traffic.

"When do we hit the dirt road?" I asked.

"A piece further," Ambrose said. "It'll be all right. Ain't been much rain recently. When the rains come, there ain't much can get through this way except a mule or a man."

"You mean you two walk it every day?"

"Nope. Just when there's a lot of rain. Then we take the long way. I got an old truck, and the trip takes longer, but the road's pretty good till we get right near the mine before we hit a dirt road. Then we have to walk a good piece. Won't have to today. The dirt road'll be in good shape, and we can drive right up to the mine entrance. A long time ago somebody put some gravel on that road, but most of it has sunk in the mud by now."

"Sounds just like civilization," I said dryly.

We soon reached the dirt road, but Ambrose had been right. It wasn't bad, but I had to keep a close watch on it and try not to go too fast. They didn't talk any, and I was watching the road, so the only sound was made by the car.

I didn't even look at my watch, but it was a long drive. My shoulders were getting tired before Ambrose spoke again. "It's just a piece now."

"Everything is just a piece to you. What's there? The mine?"

"Nope. That'll be Poeville."

"Poeville?" I said. "You mean there's a town there?"

"Not exactly. Used to be a pretty busy town, named after John Poe, who discovered the gold on the slopes of Peavine

Mountain. But there ain't been nothing there for ninety years or more except for some rocks and sometimes bits of rotted timbers. But that's where we turn for the Lucky Goddess."

He was right. There wasn't anything there, but the road was better than the dirt track we'd left behind us. There were a lot of holes and bumps in it, but you could miss most of them. Then I spotted a dirt road leading off to the right.

"That's it," Ambrose said.

I turned into it, but it wasn't much of a road. The dirt was dry, however, so it wasn't much worse than we had been on for more hours than I cared to think about. We were climbing again, and on one side of the jeep there were only a few inches before it seemed to drop straight down. On the other side there was a span of bushes and then the mountain went up. Almost straight up.

"Around that bend ahead," Ambrose said, "and we'll be there."

I made the turn, and there in front of us was a sort of plateau. There were two spots, close together, which were obviously the entrances to two mines. One was open and the other had a heavy wooden gate over the opening. There was a powerful-looking truck standing in front of the open mine. Beyond it, near the opening, there was a man sitting on a stool. He stood up at the sight of us. I could see he was holding a sawed-off shotgun.

I stopped the jeep in front of the other mine, and Ambrose and Necktie scrambled out. I picked up my bag and followed them.

"Howdy," Ambrose called to the man with the gun.

"What the hell are you doing here?" the man demanded. He had a hard, flat voice. "Too late for you to start grubbing in there, ain't it?"

"Ain't doing no digging today," Ambrose said cheerfully. "Just brought a friend of ours up to see the mine."

"Yours or ours?"

"The Lucky Goddess. Ain't much interested in yours."

"A good thing for you." The man shifted his gun slightly in our direction. His gaze shifted to me. "Who are you?"

"A friend." I wasn't giving any free information. I knew what he was, so he must be one of the partners of the other mine or a hired gun.

He shifted the shotgun again. "What's your name—friend?"

"I haven't heard your name yet. In fact, we haven't been introduced."

"Ain't that too bad." His voice was harder. "Who are you?"

"Milo March."

"Milo March? Never heard of you."

"That's just as well. It may help you to sleep better."

"What kind of crack is that? Wait a minute." His gaze had dropped to my chest. "You're carrying a piece, ain't you?"

"I've heard it called that."

"Why?"

"I like it."

"I don't." There was a click as he pulled back the hammer on the shotgun. "Maybe you think you could get it out and use it before I could pull this trigger?"

"I could try," I said gently. "You're getting nervous, chum." He hesitated, trying to make up his mind. The effort was enough to make the knuckle on his trigger finger whiten. I watched him closely.

FOUR

The long silence was finally broken by a voice shouting from inside the mine.

"Hey, Nick?"

"Yeah?" the shotgun man called back.

"You talking to yourself again?"

"No. Them two old desert rats are here again. But this time they got a smart-ass with them. Says he's a friend."

"So what? They don't tell us what to do and we don't tell them what to do. As long as they stay off our property, we leave them alone. You know that."

"Yeah, but the friend is carrying iron."

"Maybe he's afraid of snakes."

"Maybe." The gunman gave me his full attention again. "Is that right, Mac? You afraid of snakes?"

"I'm not exactly afraid of snakes—or rats," I said evenly. "I'm just careful. If it's raining, I wear a raincoat."

"Knock it off, Nick," the voice said again from inside the mine.

He lowered the hammer on the gun and waved it toward the other mine. "You heard what the man said. Go on in and drool over the little pile of gold they got. Maybe I'll see you again."

"You might at that. I'll be around. Come on, Ambrose."

I led the way to the closed mine and waited while Ambrose

unlocked the big padlock. We walked inside and waited while Ambrose closed the gate.

"Wait a minute," he said. "I'll get some light. Can't see your hand in front of your face in here." He shuffled off in the darkness. A moment later there was a light showing from an adjoining chamber and Ambrose reappeared carrying a carbide lantern.

"Got anything to sit on?" I asked.

He looked surprised. "Got two stools and an empty keg. Reckon that'll do." He disappeared again but soon was back carrying the stools and the keg. He put them on the floor.

"Thought you wanted to see the gold," Necktie said. "If you just wanted to talk about it, we could've just as well stayed in the bar. I sure could use a drink about now."

"That's what I had in mind," I told him. I sat down on a stool and put the bag down. I pulled out the three glasses and the bottle of bourbon. "After that warm welcome from your neighbor, I thought you might like a nip or two."

"Yowee," said Necktie. "We met us a live one for sure this time. I ain't even going to miss the ice. That danged Jed puts too much ice in the drinks anyway."

"It was mighty nice of you, Milo," Ambrose said, "but it wasn't exactly necessary."

"Didn't think it was. But that was a long trip between water holes for me. I thought you might like to join me." I handed each of them a glass, opened the bottle, and handed it to Ambrose. "Necktie, you won't have to worry about the ice cubes. You'll find the bourbon about the same temperature as ice." They both poured generous drinks and handed the bottle back to me. I poured about the same amount into my glass and held it up. "Let's drink to the confusion of our enemies."

"I'll drink to that," said Ambrose.

"Me, too," Necktie joined in.

"Well," I said, putting my glass down, "that was quite a welcome from your neighbor. What's his name?"

"Nick Lancer," said Ambrose. "He's one of the owners. He ain't exactly a welcoming committee. Neither are the other two. But we were standing on our own property, so I didn't figure he'd get too hairy."

"Milo got pretty hairy himself," Necktie said. He looked at me curiously. "Did you think he wouldn't pull that trigger?"

"I thought he wouldn't—unless he was pushed too far. The idea was to push him just far enough and leave it like that. I knew that none of them wanted any killings there. It might have put them out of business. If he had killed me, he would have had to kill both of you so there would be no witnesses. He knew I had a gun, but he couldn't be sure about either of you. One of you could have shot him while he was shooting me."

"We didn't have any guns," Ambrose said.

"But he couldn't be sure," I pointed out.

"How come you wanted to push him?" asked Ambrose.

"To make him nervous and uncertain. When a man gets like that, he nearly always makes a lot of mistakes. And I don't like guys like him."

"I guess he knows that by now," Necktie said. He sounded almost as excited as a little boy at his first rodeo. "It was almost like the big showdowns in the real old days around here."

"You don't know nothin' about them," Ambrose said. "You was too little."

"But my pappy told me about them when I was a little shaver."

"Your pappy was too busy predicting things to tell you about happenings he didn't know anything about hisself." He turned his head toward me. "Mind if I ask you a question, Milo?"

"Go ahead, Ambrose." I passed the bottle around and we all poured another drink. I lit a cigarette and waited.

"We met you in the bar today," he said slowly, "and had a couple of drinks together. You was interested in gold mines and we talked some, mostly about this mine. Then you wanted to know about the Natural Mine which is next door. After you heard that, you wanted to know if you could come up and see the one I own. We invited you up for this afternoon. I've been thinking about that and your little spat with Nick Lancer. You picked that without knowing who he was except that he was guarding the mine. And you carried a gun up here. It seems to me that you are a mite more interested in the Natural Mine than you are in seeing the Lucky Goddess."

I poured myself another drink and handed the bottle to Necktie.

"There are two answers to that," I said, "both of them true. I am, I admit, more directly interested in the Natural Mine. I want to find out everything I can about it and what's going on with it. There's something wrong with the setup. That's why I'm here. Some of the information I can probably get around town, but it seems rather clear that there is no way I can get inside their mine, so I have to dig up or dream up that end of it."

"You a mining engineer or something?" Necktie asked.

I shook my head. "All I know is that gold is found in rocks in the ground and that it's valuable. If I found a ton of it, I wouldn't know where to sell it, how much I could get for it, or even how to get it out of the rocks. I wouldn't know the difference between a gold nugget and a chunk of iron pyrite.* All I do know is that I'd get tired of sitting around looking at it. I'd rather have good old American paper money. I'd know what it was worth and where to spend it."

"And your other interest?" Ambrose asked.

"I have to learn as much as I can in a short period of time about what you do when you find gold. Do you just carry big boulders down the mountain and sell them? If not, how do you get the gold out of the rocks and where do you sell it? How do you find gold in a mine where there isn't any?"

"I guess we can tell you the answers to one or two of them, but not all," Ambrose said. He sounded more relaxed. "You still want to see inside where the gold is?"

"Yes. At the present I wouldn't know gold in its natural state if I ran into it. For all I know, I may have been bumping into gold all of my life without realizing it. But I do know one thing about gold, which I read a long time ago."

"What was that?" Ambrose asked.

"It was what King Ferdinand of Spain told the men he sent

---

* Otherwise known as fool's gold because of its resemblance to the real thing.

off to the Caribbean Islands in fifteen hundred and some-thing."

"He knew about gold?" Necktie asked.

"Enough to know that he wanted as much of it as he could get. It was all he needed to know. Things haven't changed much for anyone since then. 'Get gold,' he wrote to his men, 'humanely if you can, but at all hazards get gold.'* He was a man of few words."

"Want to go look at some?" Ambrose asked.

"Yes."

I stood up and followed them into the other chamber. The ceiling was braced with timbers, and the walls were uneven where rocks had been dug out. The walls were black in color, and water seeping from the top made them glisten in the light.

"There's a lot of different minerals in these rocks," Ambrose was saying, "and that's what makes them turn black from the water. But the mineral content is not large enough to make it worth digging for them." He stepped over to one wall and held the light up. I followed, noticing the picks, crowbars, sledgehammer, and hand drills on the floor. "Here's where Necktie and I have been digging for a long time."

"I don't see any gold."

"Right here," he said, putting up his hand. "Look a bit closer."

I stepped closer and looked near his hand. Finally, I saw thin streaks of yellow running through the rock. I guessed it was gold, but it didn't send any thrills through me.

---

* The Spanish empire depended on New World gold, and despite the exhortation to be "humane," the conquistadors enslaved, tortured, and murdered indigenous peoples of North and South America.

"Doesn't look like you could get much gold out of that," I said.

"Stand out of the way for a minute," he said. "I'll show you something."

I stepped back and waited. He reached for the pickax and swung it. The point stuck a couple of inches into the rock. He freed it and struck again. He repeated this several times, finally stopping to take a closer look at the rock. He struck once more, then forced down on the handle, causing it to act as a pry.

"There she comes," exclaimed Necktie. Just as he said it, a chunk of rock fell out and landed on the floor. Ambrose stepped well back and glanced at me.

"Pick it up," he said to me, "and look it over."

The piece of rock was a little larger than a baseball. I picked it up and turned it around slowly in my hands. There were yellow streaks on all sides of it, some of them fairly wide. To my surprise I felt a wave of excitement.

"All those streaks are gold?" I asked.

"Every one of them. That's a small hunk of rock, but that's good gold in it."

"How much is that worth?"

"Not very much. The rock is too small. Here, why don't you take it back to New York with you as a souvenir?" He handed it to me.

"Thanks, Ambrose," I said as I took it. "I'll always think of you and Necktie when I look at it. What do you do to get the gold out? Take it to a smelter?"

"No. Too far away. We do the work right here."

"Where? I don't see any machinery."

"In there," he said pointing. I noticed there was another hole in the chamber which I hadn't seen before. It was too dark to tell anything about it. "Anyway, it ain't exactly a machine."

"What is it, then?"

"We do it another way. It's cheaper and does just as good in a mine, especially if you're not too big. Want to see it?"

"I guess not. I wouldn't know any more after seeing it than I know now."

"Probably just as well. It's getting a little late, and I figure we'll go back the long way so we can be over the roughest part by the time it gets dark."

"Suits me," I said.

We walked back toward the front. I picked up the bag I'd brought and put the rock in it.

"Don't you want your bottle?" Necktie asked.

"Leave it here. You might get thirsty when you're digging. Let's go."

Ambrose put out the lantern and opened the door covering the entrance. We stepped outside and he locked the door. I noticed that the man was back sitting on his stool, the shotgun across his knees.

"Well," he said mockingly, "did you boys strike it rich today?"

"We did well enough," I said. "I found it very interesting. Would you like to show us through your mine?"

"We ain't running no peep show."

"No? I thought that would be more in your line."

"Knock it off," he said roughly. "You planning on visiting up here with your friends anymore?"

"I might."

"Well, if you stay on their property and keep your mouth shut, we might put up with it. We might. Or I might look you up in town and teach you some Western manners. On my own time."

"That's mighty neighborly of you," I said. "I'm staying at the Pony Express Hotel. Make it anytime. I'll even return the favor. If you're ever in the East, I'll look you up."

"You talk pretty big, but we might change that before you leave. If you do. I ain't planning on going East."

"You can never tell. They might decide to send you to a Federal slammer in the East. If you live long enough. Let's go, Ambrose."

I turned away and the three of us got in the jeep and started down the road.

"Do we turn right when we get to where the old town was?"

"Yeah," Ambrose said. "You know, you ought to be careful, Milo. You might push that Lancer too far. He's a mean one."

"I want to push him—and his friends—too far. Maybe they'll make a mistake then."

"He sure is a mean one," Necktie said. "One time when Ambrose was already at the mine, I came up by myself. He was setting on that chair of his, cleaning a handgun. I said howdy to him and I'll be danged if he didn't put a bullet right next to my feet. Thought it was funny, too."

We reached the hard road and I made the right turn, then settled down to trying to make as much time as possible.

There wasn't much talking, and I drove as fast as the conditions would permit.

It was a longer way back to Reno, but we probably made it in about the same time, or less, because we didn't have to take any dirt roads. It was completely dark when we hit the outskirts of Reno, but it wasn't late.

"Name your bar," I said, "and I'll buy the drinks."

"That's mighty kind of you," Ambrose said, "but me and Necktie are a mite tired and it's easier to just go home. If you wanted to ask any more questions, you're welcome to stop for a spell."

"I would like to for just a minute," I said. "I won't stay long and I'll stop on only one condition. If you let me buy you some refreshment to take along."

"Reckon that would be all right," Ambrose said.

They told me where to stop. As I got out of the car, I asked if there was anything else I could get them. Ambrose said there wasn't. I went inside and bought a half gallon of bourbon and some ice cubes. I carried the bag out to the car and got behind the wheel.

"Where to?" I asked.

They gave me directions and I soon pulled up in front of an old house. It was small and looked as if it had outlived its time. We went inside. The furniture was all old, but everything in the house was clean. I handed the bag to Necktie, who disappeared with it into the kitchen.

"Wash the glasses," Ambrose called after him. "We might as well sit down, Milo. Necktie ain't much good in the kitchen, but he pours a good drink and don't take long at it."

"I only have two or three questions, Ambrose," I said. "Then I'll go on to the hotel and let you two hit the sack."

"Yeah, we could use it. But first let's sit down a spell and get the weight off our bones. Then we'll oil our throats with some of that bourbon and we can talk."

Necktie entered with three glasses full of bourbon and ice. He put them down on the table and pulled up a chair. He picked up a glass and lifted it. "Mud in your eye," he said. We all drank.

"Before you ask your questions, Milo," Ambrose said, "I'd like to know something."

"That's fair enough. Go ahead." I took out a cigarette and lit it.

Ambrose nodded, a serious look on his face. "Me and Necktie met you for the first time today in a bar. You said you was interested in gold mines and asked some questions. We told you that I owned a mine and you wanted to know if we knew anything about the Natural. I said it was right next to mine and you got more interested and right away wanted to visit my mine. We agreed to take you up to see it today. Right?"

"Right," I agreed.

"That fellow Nick was out front as usual. At least, one of them is always out there riding shotgun. He got curious about you and you took a dislike to him. We went into the mine and you asked a few questions, but you didn't ask the kind you would've if you'd been real interested in gold mining. It struck me then that you was a mite more interested in that particular mine than in just any mine. Was I right?"

"You were right," I said.

"You never did tell us what kind of work you do or why you're in Reno. I'd kind of like to know that. And why you're interested in the Natural Mine."

"Fair enough. I'm an insurance investigator. I'm in Reno working on a case. I carry a gun, and have a license to carry it, because of my work." I lifted the glass and took another drink.

"Insurance investigator? What do you do?"

"If someone has a policy with my company and is trying to collect on it, it is my job to go out and find out if there's fraud in it. Or is somebody trying to steal the money."

"The Natural Mine? How much money?"

"The Natural. Two million dollars."

Ambrose took another healthy drink. "That's a lot of money. How would they steal it?"

"The insurance company insured them against the mine running out of gold. They claim it has. So they want the money."

"That's fraud?"

"That's one word for it," I said. "Conspiracy to defraud. Your namesake, Ambrose Bierce, called it absconding, which he said was 'to "move in a mysterious way," commonly with the property of another.'* No matter what word you use, it's stealing."

"How can they do it?"

"That's what I'm here to find out. But remember, I don't want either of you to say a word about this to anybody. I don't

---

* That was Bierce's definition of *abscond*, in which he quotes from a popular phrase, "God moves in mysterious ways." But Bierce actually defined *fraud* satirically as "the life of commerce, the soul of religion, the bait of courtship and the basis of political power."

mind if they find out who I am and why I'm here, but I want them to find out in my way and at my time."

"We won't say nothing," Ambrose said. "Will we, Necktie?"

"You can bet your last pair of pants we won't," Necktie said. It was easy to guess that was a big bet for him. He was probably wearing his last pair of pants, but to him it seemed sensible to buy whiskey with his money and another pair when they were finished.

"How do you figure they're cheatin' you?" Ambrose asked.

"I don't know the method they're using, but I know that they have to be salting the mine in some fashion."

"Who made the assay?"

"Smith."

"I told you I don't trust that man."

"There's only one thing wrong with that. They didn't hire Smith. He was hired by a man the insurance company sent out to check."

"Well, I don't trust him."

"I don't trust any of them, Ambrose. I'll even check on the day they claim they were born. I know that our man hired Smith. That's all. It doesn't rule anyone out."

"I just don't like him. Did he go look at the mine or did he just look at a piece of rock they brought in?"

"According to my information, he went to the mine and took several sample specimens. His report was that there was between four and five million dollars' worth of gold in the mine."

"Balderdash," snorted Ambrose. "There ain't that much gold in the whole mountain. Ain't no way they could salt a mine to make it show a sampling that would make such a report reasonable."

"I believe you, but I have to prove it. You got any idea how they could salt a mine that heavily?"

Ambrose shook his head. "They'd have to get enough gold embedded in the rock to make an estimate of four million dollars. It would have to look natural and be high-grade ore. I don't see no way. Do you, Necktie?"

"Nope."

"All right," I said. "Let's suppose they could get Smith or someone else to make a false report. Even if they offered him a million dollars to do it, wouldn't the report of another assayer prove that the first report had been deliberately false?"

"Yeah. Reckon you might have to get a court order or something like that."

"I'm not ready to try that yet," I said. "Tell me again how you get the gold out of the ore. Wouldn't it be easier and faster to take it to the nearest smelter?"

"Yeah, but it would cost too much for a small mine. Far as I know, the nearest smelter is at Ely. You'd have to freight the ore out of the mountain and deliver it to Ely. That would be expensive, and you still have to pay the smelting cost. A small mine couldn't make much."

"How about a mine as large as the Natural?"

"Wouldn't rightly pay them either. That's considered a small mine. Nothing like the mines in the days when the big strikes were hit around here."

I lit another cigarette and thought a minute. "All right. Tell me how you get the gold out of the ore."

"There are three ways. There's a smelter and a stamp mill. And there's what we use. It's called a melter. All you need is copper sheeting, mercury, plenty of water, a wire sieve, a heavy sledgehammer, and the muscles to swing it. You sluice it down with water, separating the gold from the bits of rock."

"Does the Natural also use that method?"

"They must. They don't haul any ore out of it. And it leaves them a bigger profit."

"Now, what do you do when you have the gold separated?"

"Me and Necktie, we just carry it down out of the mountain. We sell it to a gold broker."

"In Reno?"

"Yeah, there's one in Reno."

"What about the Natural?"

"Well, I ain't seen them doing it, but I figure they're melting it and molding it into bars. I guess the days when they mold, they take it out of the mountain in that truck you saw. They probably sell it in Frisco."

"Wouldn't a million dollars in gold make a big, heavy load?"

"Not big. I read somewhere that a million dollars in gold would look like a puffed-up yellow cushion on a footstool. Less than two feet high."

"How heavy?"

"About twenty-two hundred pounds or a ton."

"Ever see them loading their truck?"

He shook his head. "They make all the trips at night."

"How much work do you and Necktie put in?"

"Well, we usually work three days and take a day off. Then

another three days and a day off. That's enough work for us and, like I told you, we get enough money to live on."

"How much do they work in the other mine?"

"At first they usually worked about a half day and left in the evening. Lately they been putting in a full day, usually four of them. That means three of them working and one on guard. I don't rightly know when they leave. Sometimes we stay up there until after dark, and they always leave a while after we've left."

"All right. That's enough for now." I finished my drink and stood up. "I want to ask one more favor. Some night soon, when you don't have to work the next day, would you and Necktie take me back up to your mine? I'd like it to be while they're still there."

"Reckon we can," Ambrose said. "We'd have to leave the car this side of the bend and walk the rest of the way. We could hide the car in that high shrubbery to one side of the road and then come back down after they leave. That the way you want it?"

"That's the way," I said. "Thanks, boys."

"Don't you want another drink?" Necktie asked. He sounded eager, as though he thought I might take the bottle away with me.

"Not now. Keep it here. Good night."

They both said good night and I left. Outside I got into the jeep and headed for town. I parked the car at the hotel and went in. Upstairs in my room, I stripped off my clothes and took a shower. I put on a pair of slacks and a sport shirt, put the bag containing the chunk of gold ore in the closet, and went downstairs to the bar.

I had one martini in the bar, then went into the dining room, where I had another drink and a good steak dinner. I picked up the evening newspaper and went back to my room.

The news was about like anywhere else. There were reports of local and national muggings. Someone had tried to hijack a plane. Politicians were still calling each other names. It was like a gun fight without any bullets. On the local scene, some lady had won a slot machine jackpot for five thousand dollars.

The telephone rang. I walked over to it, picked up the receiver, and said hello.

"March?" a man's voice asked.

"I'm March. Who are you?"

"Someone who wants to do you a favor." I'd had calls like that before.

"Don't try too hard," I said. "You might give yourself a hernia. Who's this? The smart-ass?"

"Never mind who I am, March. You ever hear of Angelo Bacci?"

I remembered him. He was a big-shot hood. Lived in Florida. Was an important man in the Syndicate. I'd had some business with him on my last case.

"I've heard of him," I said. "Seems to me that he once did some time here in Nevada. Don't tell me he's back here trying for another spin of the wheel? I didn't know the punk had that much guts."

"You're mixed up, March. In this case, you're the punk."

"I recognize your dulcet tones now. You're the one who's a big man with a shotgun. You want to be careful you don't shoot yourself in the foot. Tell Angelo that if he has any of his boys around, he better take out some insurance on them. That way they won't be a total loss. If he takes out some on himself, his widow might appreciate it. Is that all you want to tell me?"

"No," he said angrily. "There's a plane leaving Reno at nine-thirty tomorrow morning. Be on it, punk."

There was a click as he hung up. It was starting out as a friendly evening.

The phone rang again. Maybe he had forgotten part of the message. I picked up the receiver. "It's your dime," I said.

"Milo?" It was a girl's voice. That was an improvement.

"I hope so," I said. "Who's this?"

"Rusty Lane." That was the name of the girl who had been my stewardess on the flight out. "I'm in Reno, and you promised to buy me a martini if I was here."

"Several martinis and a dinner. Where are you?"

"The Mapes."

"I'll be there in an hour, honey." I hung up.

Some days are like that. You get some bad news and then some good news. It balances out.

FIVE

It turned out to be quite a night—in more ways than one. I shaved and changed clothes again. I looked through the paper to see if there was a good show at one of the casinos. There were several, but I picked the Ames Brothers.* I called and made a reservation.

Rusty was ready when I arrived. I phoned from the lobby and she said she'd be right down. She was, too. She was more beautiful than I remembered her. It must have been the dress she was wearing. I concluded that the airline uniforms were too much of a cover-up and decided to write a letter about it when I got back home.

The other casino was only a block away, so we walked to it. On the way, I suddenly remembered that I'd already had dinner. Oh, well, I could pick at something and say I was on a diet.

The dining room was doing a good business, but it wasn't crowded. As the maître d' started to lead us to a table, I slipped him enough to make sure that we got a good one. It takes talent to be a good maître d' or headwaiter. I've never

---

* The Ames Brothers were a very successful pop quartet of the 1950s, before rock and roll took over. The brothers were middle-aged at the time of Milo's date with Rusty, but then Milo himself was already 54 in 1972, the probable year of this story (first published 1973). His age is not mentioned here, but he was 34 in the initial book of the series, *Hangman's Harvest* (1952).

seen one look at a bill, so they must be able to tell the amount by feeling the money. This one was especially talented. He didn't look down, but he shifted direction without losing a step and led us to a table which was almost on the stage. I ordered two martinis, and he glided away.

"You didn't mind that I called?" she asked.

"Well ... ," I said, "I had been thinking of running out and hijacking a plane, but I guess I'm getting a little tired of that. I need a new hobby."

"I thought you were working."

"I am, I am. But I'm tired of that hobby, too. Now that I've seen you, maybe I'll take up girls. I never thought of them before."

"I'll bet! You're really working?"

"I worked all day," I said indignantly.

The martinis arrived and we waited until the waiter had left. I lifted my glass. "Here's to working like this every day."

She drank and set her glass down. "Did you *really* work all day?"

"Of course."

"What did you do?"

"Well, I drove two old prospectors and myself up Peavine Mountain in a jeep, and we sat around all afternoon in an old gold mine and drank bourbon. It was very good bourbon. I had been thoughtful enough to pack dry ice around it, so it was as cold as it should be without all those noisy ice cubes banging around in the glass."

"That was all?"

"That was enough. Did you ever drive a jeep all the way

up a mountain just to drink bourbon? It's tiring. But that was only half of the day. I then drove us back down the mountain and stopped at the house where the men live and had more bourbon."

"Do you call that working?"

"I certainly do. And that wasn't the finish of the day. I then drove on to my hotel and carried a rock filled with streaks of gold up to my room."

She laughed. "Do you mean you get paid for that?"

"I earned three hundred dollars today," I said stiffly. "That's enough to take you out to dinner tonight. It's nothing to scoff at."

"I wasn't scoffing," she said. "I just think it's silly and you made the whole thing up. What did you really do?"

"I told you. The only thing I left out was that earlier today I met the two old prospectors in a bar and passed a few pleasant bowls with them, talking about their mine. It's called the Lucky Goddess. Then I rented a jeep, and the rest of the day you know about."

"Is that your business? You work for somebody who's going to open a gold mine out here?"

"No. I work for somebody who's going to close a gold mine out here."

"You're kidding! Who would want to do that?"

"The company I work for."

"Why do they want to do that?"

"I guess you were telling the truth when you told me you always ask questions," I said, sighing. "They want to close the gold mine because unless it's done very soon, they're going to lose two million dollars. That's against their religion."

"Do you mean there isn't any gold in the mine and that's why they will lose two million dollars?"

"No," I said patiently. "I don't know how much gold is in the mine, but I do know there's a lot of gold coming out of the mine. And that's going to cost them two million dollars."

She gulped the rest of her martini. "I'm getting dizzy and it's not from the martini. I want another one."

"That's the first time you haven't asked a question since we sat down," I said. I caught the waiter's eye and held up my empty glass. He nodded and scurried away. She stared at me moodily until he returned with the drinks. I raised my fresh glass. "To the confusion of our enemies."

"I'm not your enemy," she said seriously. She took a big swallow of her drink. "Let's start all over again. Who do you work for?"

"An insurance company. A big one. They have so much money they could buy every working gold mine around here and never miss it."

"And they are involved somehow in a mine that's producing a lot of gold, but they're going to lose two million dollars. The only thing I believe is the part about the bourbon." She took a deep breath. It was a beautiful view. "Does the insurance company own the mine?"

"No."

"Did they loan someone the money to open the mine?"

"No."

"Then how the hell are they going to lose two million dollars?"

"Not so loud," I said. "Everybody will want part of the action."

"All right," she said in defeat. "I'll promise not to ask any questions if you promise to tell me anything that makes sense."

"That sounds fair enough. I'll start at the beginning. I work for Intercontinental Insurance. They were founded in—"

"Don't start so far back," she said. "Just tell me the part that applies to your presence in Reno."

"Well, at least you know who I work for. Some time ago, a group of men acquired possession of a gold mine up in the mountain. They named it the Natural Gold Mine and incorporated it. They applied to my company for an insurance policy which, in the event that the mine ran dry—or whatever it is that a mine does when it no longer has any gold in it—before they had taken two million dollars in gold from the mine, guaranteed that the company would pay them two million dollars."

"Minus what gold they had taken out?"

"No. That was their second mistake."

"What was the first mistake?"

"Agreeing to insure them in the first place. My job is to protect them from their own mistakes, even though they don't consult me in advance. They have a bunch of little men who work on a straight salary, and if they aren't working, the company is losing money. So they use them in the beginning and then yell for help when something goes wrong. And that is why I'm here working."

"Is that why you're carrying the gun that you said was in your luggage in New York?"

"That's the reason."

"It must be very dangerous."

"It's very dangerous to take a shower in your bathroom, if you slip. Most things aren't dangerous unless you slip."

"And you're supposed to save their money for them?"

"That's the general idea."

"Do you think you can?"

"Sure."

"How are you going to do it?"

"I have one simple approach to problems like this. The people who try to take insurance companies for large amounts of money are usually professional crooks. First I learn who is involved. Then I start pushing them a little. That makes them think I know more than I do, and they try to push back even harder. Then I just wait until they slip. That's all there is to it. But don't give away my secret."

"I won't. But—"

"That's all," I interrupted. "I didn't make a date with you so I could talk about dear old Intercontinental. I'm fond of them, but not that fond. How long are you staying in Reno?"

"Just tonight."

"Then back to San Francisco?"

"No. I have two weeks of vacation coming, so I'm going on to New York tomorrow morning, just to enjoy myself for the two weeks."

"That sounds like fun. I might be back there before your two weeks are up. Maybe I could tag along some night."

"I'd like that," she said.

"All right. Now let's talk about you."

So we talked about her. It was more interesting than I had expected it to be. We stopped long enough to order dinner. All that talk had made me hungry again, so I ordered a rare filet mignon for myself, no salad and no vegetables. A good balanced dinner.

The show came on and that stopped the talking for a while. It was a good show.

Finally we had coffee and brandy, and then she wanted to go gamble. Her idea of gambling was a slot machine. Mine was the dice table. She won a four-hundred dollar jackpot, and I lost a hundred dollars. It was very late and I decided that it must be time for dessert.

We went back to the Mapes. We were standing in front of the elevators and suddenly she stretched up and kissed me lightly on the mouth.

"I had a wonderful time, Milo," she said. "It was just like a real date. I do hope I see you in New York. I'm not sure which hotel I'll be at. Shall I call you at the insurance company? The Intercontinental?"

"Yeah," I said. "That's a good idea, Rusty. You call me at the insurance company. They'll know if I'm back yet."

The elevator doors opened and she stepped inside. "Good night, Milo."

"Good night," I muttered.

The elevator boy was staring at me with a surprised expression on his face. If he'd smiled, I'd have given him something to be surprised about—his teeth down his throat.

"Arthritis," I murmured instead and turned and hobbled outdoors. Then I straightened up and hurried to a taxi parked in front of the hotel. On the way, I remembered that Mei Hsu would be arriving in a day or two. Riding in the cab, I told myself that I was a virtuous, faithful man of strong moral fiber. By the time I reached the hotel, I believed it myself. I went straight upstairs and went to bed. It had been a big day.

I was up early the next morning. First I made myself a glass of gin and orange juice. Then I called room service. The juice had been by the window all night and was pretty cold. It tasted great. By the time it was finished, I was ready for breakfast. I poured another drink and put the gin and orange juice in a dresser drawer.

When the knock on the door came, I was almost ready for the day. I opened the door and the waiter came in. He put the tray with the morning paper on the table near the window and presented me with the check. As he did so, his gaze fell on my glass half full of what he thought was orange juice.

"If you had told me you wanted juice," he said reproach-fully, "I would have brought you a fresh glass."

"I already had some," I said. "I often wake up in the middle of the night and need some orange juice before I can go back to sleep. It's easier than calling room service and I get back to sleep quicker." I took the check, added a tip, and signed it. The waiter glanced at the tip, then wished me a good day with a big smile. It was so easy to make him happy.

I finished breakfast, then picked up the Reno telephone directory. I sorted out Manfred Smith's name from all the other Smiths and made a note of his address. It was in the center of the downtown area. I threw a dirty shirt in the closet so that it covered the package with the gold ore. I went downstairs. It wasn't quite ten o'clock. I decided it was a little early to see Smith. I had noticed that the most affluent lawyers quite often reached their offices a little late.

The cashier gave me two handfuls of silver dollars in exchange for two tens, and I walked over to the dollar slot machine and started feeding it. I made a couple of small hits, but my supply of silver dollars was diminishing. Finally, I glanced at my watch and decided it was time to go. I put another dollar in the machine and pulled the handle. I stood there and watched three symbols line up like little soldiers and then the bell went off.

A group of people suddenly formed around me, staring at the three symbols. There are interesting things to see in a casino, especially around the slots. If you play the big machines, even the ones that take a half dollar, there will always be quite a number of people watching you. If you hit, more hurry over to share in the vicarious thrill of seeing you paid off. Invariably, they are the ones who will never gamble that much. Once someone hits a jackpot, one of them may make a play or two, but that's all.

My favorites, though, are the little old ladies who play the nickel or dime machines and usually play three machines at a time. They carry their money in a paper drinking cup. They place a coin in one machine and pull the handle, then rush to the second machine and do the same, and on to the third and repeat the play. By then it's time to rush back to the first one. They will keep this up for hours. No matter how often they hit, I don't think I've ever seen one pick up her money and leave. Hardy and optimistic souls.

The man finally came, made a note of the amount, and shut off the bell. Telling me he'd be right back, he walked away, leaving me and my admirers waiting. Finally he returned, made me sign a receipt, and gave me a check for three hundred dollars. That was so I would have to declare it on my income tax. I took one more dollar and put it in the machine, playing off the jackpot. That's an unwritten, often broken law of slot machines.

I cashed the check and went out to the LTD. I drove downtown and parked in a parking lot. I put seventy-five cents in a machine and received a ticket which entitled me to play one free game of twenty-one. Even parking is a gambling game.

Smith's office was in a three-story building on South Virginia Street. He was on the second floor. I walked up and entered the office. There was an attractive girl sitting at the desk.

"Hello," she said, smiling. "May I help you?"

"That depends," I said. "How about lunch?"

The smile became a laugh. "I never go out with clients."

"I'm not a client yet. While you're making up your mind, may I see Mr. Smith?"

She reached for the phone. "Your name?"

"Milo March."

"Your business?"

"I want to talk to him about a gold mine."

"I'll see if he has time, Mr. March," she said. That meant he was probably sitting in his private office playing solitaire. She picked up the phone and announced me and my business. She listened for a moment and replaced the receiver. "You're lucky. He's free and he'll see you. Right through that door."

I opened the door and stepped inside. The office was expensively furnished. The walls were hung with good pictures and two or three diplomas. The middle-aged man behind the desk was well dressed and smooth-looking. Almost too smooth.

"I'm Manfred Smith," he said, standing up and holding out his hand. We shook hands. His grip was that of a man who thinks he has to break your fingers to prove he's a man. "Sit down, Mr. March, and tell me what I can do for you."

I sat down. "You're an attorney?"

"Yes."

"And a gold assayer?"

"Yes. Are you interested in gold?"

"You might say that. I'd like some general information about gold mines, especially information about one specific gold mine."

His face took on the expression of a bird who has just seen a cat sneaking up on him and is prepared. "Which one?"

"The Natural Gold Mine. I believe you know it."

He nodded. "What is the nature of the information you want? I might be able to help you if it doesn't affect a client of mine."

"If you don't have more than one client, I am a part of that client," I said. "You made an assay report on the mine."

"Yes, I did. For Intercontinental Insurance, I believe."

"I work for them," I said. I took out my card case and handed it to him. My ID was behind one window and my Nevada gun permit was behind the other. I had arranged it that way intentionally before I left the hotel.

"An insurance investigator?" he said, pushing it back to me. "Does that mean there's something wrong?"

"It might. I'd like to hear about your assay report."

"You think there's something wrong with it?" he asked with an edge of heat.

"I wouldn't know if there was anything wrong with it if I were looking right at it," I said with a smile. "I merely want you to tell me what you found—in language I can understand."

He returned my smile and seemed to relax. "I took several samplings and examined them very carefully. It was high-grade ore. It was a good vein and ran as far as I could examine. The vein was still large, and the logical assumption was that it would continue for a considerable distance. I believe I estimated it would produce at least four million dollars in gold. Maybe more. It must be doing all right because I've heard that they've been sending out regular shipments of gold."

"Was the vein you examined the same one that was being worked when the mine was doing so well years ago?"

"I don't believe so. I understand that one had been exhausted when the mine was closed."

"Interesting," I said. "When you were hearing things about them, did you also hear that the vein has run out and they do not believe there's any more gold in the mine?"

"No!" He managed to sound surprised, but I didn't think it rang completely true. "They can't have taken that much gold out in this short time."

"Something less than one million dollars, I am told."

"I don't see how that's possible," he exclaimed. "The ore was— Wait a minute. You can see for yourself. I still have a small piece of the ore I examined. They gave it to me at the time." He opened a desk drawer and pulled out an object. It was a rock not much bigger than a golf ball. It was mounted on a piece of polished wood. There was a copper plate on it on which was engraved: *Natural Gold Mine—Reno.* I glanced at the rock. There were thick yellow streaks through it. I couldn't tell whether they were gold or not.

"Pretty," I said, putting it back on the desk. "You may have to put another inscription on it to make it complete. Something like: *Gold from a Mine That Has No Gold.*"

"What do you mean?"

"Well, if the mine is running out of gold, that may be a true statement before long. That should make it a late antique, worth much more than it is now."

"I think I'd better ask them if they mind if I come up and take a look at it."

"I was just about to ask you if you could do that and take me with you."

He looked worried. "I think I can arrange that. We might have to wait four or five days."

"Why?"

"I heard that they've been working night and day. If the vein is running out, they may try to be finished up soon and wouldn't want interruptions. I'll do the best I can."

"I'm sure you will," I said sweetly. I stood up. "I'm sorry to take up your time, Mr. Smith. I'll check back with you in a couple of days."

"Do that, Mr. March. I'll be glad to give you all the assistance I can."

"Thank you." I turned toward the door. As I took my first step, I heard him pick up the phone.

"Good-bye," he called as I opened the door.

"Good-bye," I called over my shoulder and closed the door. The secretary was obviously just finishing a phone conversation as I turned to her. "All right, Mr. Turner," she was saying, "I'll have him call you the first thing after lunch." She put down the receiver. "Well, that was pretty fast, Mr. March. I just finished telling a client that Mr. Smith was busy."

"It didn't take long," I said. "Did you make up your mind about lunch?"

She smiled. "Are you a client yet?"

"No. It seems that I was sort of his client once, but I'm not now."

"Then I'll be glad to have lunch with you. Will about forty-five minutes from now be all right?"

"Fine."

"Where shall I meet you?"

"How about the Waldorf? Across the street. I'll reserve a table and be waiting for you at the bar."

"I'll be there, Mr. March."

"Milo," I said. "What's your name?"

"Carol. Carol Chilton."

"Okay, Carol." I left the office and went across the street. The Waldorf had just opened. I went in and took a stool near the door. The bartender came up.

"Hello, Joe," I said.

"Hello, Milo. What'll you have? The usual?"

I nodded and he hurried off. He mixed a martini and came back to put it in front of me. Just then somebody came in and went down to the other end of the bar. Joe followed him.

I took a drink of the martini, got off the stool, and went to the phone on the wall behind me. I looked in the book. The Natural Gold Mine Corporation was listed with an address on West Second Street. I found a dime in my pocket, dropped it in the slot, and dialed the number.

"The Natural Gold Mine Corporation," a voice said. It was a girl who sounded as if she were talking around two sticks of gum.

"Mr. Mancetti, please," I said.

"He's not in."

"How about Mr. Lake or Mr. Lancer?"

"They're not in either. Who's calling?"

"My name is March. You people carry a policy with an insurance company I represent. Is there anyone there I can talk to?"

"Mr. Belli is here. He's the bookkeeper."

"Let me talk to him, then."

"Just a minute." A moment later, a man's voice answered.

"This is Dean Belli," he said. "I'm the bookkeeper. May I help you?"

"My name is Milo March," I said. "I'm here representing Intercontinental Insurance. You have a policy with us covering the Natural Gold Mine. I would like to arrange a meeting with some or all of the principals as soon as possible."

"Well," he said hesitatingly, "it is a rather difficult time. Everyone is quite busy at the moment, and I'm not certain when it could be arranged. Is it important?"

"We think so and I imagine that you should think so. We carry a policy on your mine. You have informed us that the gold in your mine seems to be exhausted and that you are therefore demanding payment of the full face value of the policy. In other words, you are asking us to give you two million dollars. Don't you think that's important, Mr. Belli?"

"Yes. Yes, of course. Does your call indicate that you are considering contesting the claim?"

"You might say that. It certainly means that we do want the answers to a number of questions, and I want to arrange to visit the mine and to bring an assayer with me. Before the mine is closed down."

"That will be most inconvenient, Mr. March. I will have to speak to the men who own the corporation."

"You do that," I said. "While you're speaking to them, you might tell them that my next move will be a damned sight more inconvenient for them. You may also tell them that I have reason to believe that they are in no position to refuse. Do you understand, Mr. Belli?"

"Yes, yes. I understand. Where can you be reached, Mr. March?"

"The Pony Express Hotel. When do you expect to see them?"

"I will try to talk to them tonight and will phone you tomorrow, or you may hear from them directly. I'm rather certain that they will be displeased at the speed you demand."

"That's too bad. If I don't hear from you early tomorrow, I will take more direct methods. Good-bye, Mr. Belli."

I hung up and went back to the bar and my martini. I was rather pleased with the phone call. That was a big enough push to cause some kind of action. All I had to do was wait.

I picked up the martini and finished it. I motioned to Joe for another.

SIX

The early-lunchers were starting to come in, so I beckoned to Joe and asked him to have one of the girls save me a table for two, preferably the first booth on the left after entering the dining room.

"Oh?" he said, his eyebrows going up suggestively. "Who are you having lunch with?"

"She says it's Carol Chilton. She works across the street. For Smith."

"Oh, yes. She's the little blonde, isn't she?"

"I guess so," I said. "Some parts of her are little and some parts aren't. All in all, it adds up to a pretty good package."

"That's the one. That expense account must come in pretty handy. Cuts down on exploring costs. How does the company take to that?"

"They take a dim view, but they don't do much except grumble once in a while.

They're smart enough to know that if you want the wild animals to do their tricks, you have to throw them a piece of raw meat once in a while."

I finished my drink and was debating if I should order another when I saw her coming in. I slid off the stool and went to meet her. She looked even better standing up.

"Did I keep you waiting?" she asked.

"If you did, it was worth every minute of it. I reserved a table for us. Let's go on back. We can get our vitamins there." I escorted her to the rear and there was a "Reserved" sign on the table I had told Joe I wanted. We sat down and the waitress came over. On the way, she took a look at the girl and nodded her approval. I began to feel like I was on exhibition.

"What's your favorite vitamin?" I asked Carol.

She smiled. "A very dry martini. Up." She certainly knew her booze.

"Make it two," I told the waitress. "No point in stopping with a winning streak going."

She went to the bar and I noticed that Joe had anticipated the order. All she had to do was pick up the two glasses and bring them back.

I lifted my glass. "To the only beautiful woman in the room."

She drank and put her glass down. "You didn't even look at the others."

"Did you ever play poker?" I asked her.

"Not much but a few times. Why?"

"If you're sitting there looking at a royal flush, you don't much care what anyone else is holding."

"You don't lose much time, do you? And I noticed that you get fast service here, so they must know you. I thought you were from out of town."

"I am, but I've been to Reno a few times. The first time I go to a new town, I try to locate a few water holes I like. Then, if I go back there, I know where to go."

"Where are you from?"

"New York."

"Are you here to gamble or on business, or both, Mr. March?" I looked around to see if there was anyone behind me. "Milo," she corrected with a smile.

"A little bit of everything," I said. "I try to go wherever the action is. It's more fun if you play everything by ear."

"That sounds exciting," she said. "But you must be interested in gold?"

"I prefer the green version of gold, but why do you ask?"

"Well, you came to see Mr. Smith and you mentioned that you used to be a client of his. He has two professions. He's a gold assayer and an attorney. You don't look like you need the latter."

"Smart as well as beautiful," I said. "I am not especially interested in gold. I don't think of myself as the prospector type. But I am interested in a particular old mine. In fact, I was once Mr. Smith's client, because I hired him to get some information for me on that mine."

"A gold mine buff?"

"Not exactly. Did you ever read anything by Robert Service?"

"I don't think so," she said. "Who is he?"

"He was a very fine poet. He wrote some lines once that are a good explanation of my attitude about this mine. He said:

"There's gold, and it's haunting and haunting;
It's luring me on as of old;
Yet it isn't the gold that I'm wanting

So much as just finding the gold."*

"It's pretty, but I don't think I understand it."

"Never mind. I'll explain it sometime." Our drinks were finished, so I motioned to the waitress to bring us two more.

"What do you do in New York?" Carol asked.

"The same thing I do here. I work for an insurance company. An insurance investigator."

"What does that mean?"

"It merely means that when someone is trying to dip their fingers into the company's till, I'm sent out to explain that it's a no-no."

"That sounds exciting. Is that why you were seeing Mr. Smith this morning?"

Our fresh martinis arrived, and I waited until the waitress had left. "That was the reason. We have insurance on the company, and Mr. Smith made an assay report on the mine at the time they applied for a policy."

"Didn't you see his report?"

"Yes. But I wanted to make sure that it was the same as the report he had in his office. Someone might have got to it and changed it before we read it."

"Did you think he might have made a dishonest report? He wouldn't do anything like that. I know he wouldn't."

---

* From "The Spell of the Yukon" (1907). The Yukon territory in northwestern Canada was the site of the Klondike gold rush in 1896–1899. Robert Service's poem tells the story of a young man who went there to seek his fortune, but after succeeding he finds that experiencing the wild beauty of the Yukon is more valuable to him than gold. For Milo, the verse has a double meaning: he is not interested in gold, but is haunted by the puzzle of how there came to be gold in a mine that had none in it.

"Of course not," I said. I was only lying a little. I knew damn well he would if the price was right and if he thought he could get away with it. I also knew something else he would do and was doing. He had picked up his phone as I started to leave his office. But he hadn't dialed, and he hadn't spoken into the phone. And Carol was on the phone in the next office when I closed the door and looked at her. She didn't say anything until she knew she had my attention. Her short remarks, which were the only ones I heard her make, could have meant that she was saying she would try to pump me and that she would have lunch with me.

I decided this just wasn't my week on the girl front. First one who just wanted to be a curious pal, and now one who was a curious spy. Well, if that was going to be Mr. Smith's game, I might as well start pushing him, too. It might be interesting.

"But why did you think the report might have been changed?" she asked.

"I didn't think it had. I just wanted to make sure that it hadn't. It's a little like looking for a needle in a haystack."

She smiled. "What does the needle represent?"

I lit a cigarette and took another drink. "Two million dollars," I said quietly, watching her eyes.

There was a slight change of expression. I thought it indicated surprise. Probably at the amount.

"Two million dollars? You mean in gold?"

"No. I mean two million dollars in good U.S. currency. It's easier to carry around than gold. Would you like another martini?"

"Well—only if we order lunch at the same time. I do have to go back to work soon. Besides, I'd hate to be counted out before the game even starts."

It was too bad that she had to be mixed up in this. She was beautiful and had a good sense of humor. That's a combination that's hard to beat. On the other hand, I didn't want to make a pass at her only to find out that she'd lifted my wallet while I was making it. Something like that takes the romance out of it.

I waved to the waitress and turned back to Carol. "It's too late, honey," I said gently. "The game has already started." I meant it in a slightly different way than she had when she used the same word. But she didn't catch the slight difference and laughed. The waitress arrived and we ordered two more martinis and lunch.

"Do you always drink that much?" she asked when the waitress was gone.

"Only when I'm where I can get it. Let me think. Yesterday was a rough day, so I had two drinks before breakfast this morning. I played the slot machines at the hotel after breakfast, just to loosen up my stiff arm, then came down to your office. When I left, I came here. I had one martini, then had a long conversation on the phone, went back to the bar, and had two more martinis while I waited for you. Then I've had the ones here with you. They shouldn't count."

"Why not?" she asked in surprise.

"I find beautiful women very sobering. If they're also intelligent, they're twice as sobering."

"You like your women to be smashed?"

"God forbid. I have very little tolerance for drunks, men or women. People who can't hold their liquor usually can't hold anything else. And in some cases, just being with one is like expecting an uncoordinated child to thread a needle."

She laughed again. "You're a strange man. Do you always keep such close count on how many drinks you have?"

"I didn't until lately. It started out as self-defense. People used to count my drinks for me and then declare that no one could drink that much. I was also constantly meeting characters in bars who would accuse me of lying about how much I drank and then would challenge me to a drinking contest. By the time the contest was over, they didn't even remember they'd been in a contest. And sometimes I had to take them home. That was too much."

The waitress arrived with the food and drinks. She winked at me and left.

"What was that for?" Carol asked.

"What was what for?"

"She winked at you."

"What bright, big eyes you have, darling," I said. "That merely meant that she approved of you. She likes to pass judgment on anyone I bring in here."

"Does she always approve?"

"I never counted. It takes too much time."

We were silent for a while as we enjoyed our lunch. Then, over coffee, Carol resumed her questioning.

"Tell me more about your job here," she said. "It sounds so fascinating."

"There's nothing to it, really," I said lightly. "All I have to do is save the company two million dollars. Anyone could do it."

"I'll bet," she said scornfully. "But how are they about to lose two million dollars? Why and to whom?"

"There are three men out here who acquired an old abandoned mine. They formed a company which is called the Natural Gold Mine Corporation. They claimed that there was at least four million dollars in gold in the mine. They applied to us for a policy which would insure them for two million dollars against the mine's prematurely running out of gold. The company sent a man out to look into it. He was a good man, but like me, he didn't know what gold looked like unless he saw it in a display case in Cartier's. So he hired an assayer Mr. Smith. The investigator and Mr. Smith got permission to go up and examine the mine. Mr. Smith wrote a report saying that there was between four and five million dollars in gold. All our man knew was that he saw a lot of rocks with yellow streaks in them. The policy was issued."

"That sounds fair enough," she said. "Mr. Smith wouldn't make up a story like that."

"I didn't say that he did. There could be other explanations. He might have made an honest error. Or someone might have gotten the report after it left his hands and before our man either looked at it or mailed it to the company in New York. Mr. Smith says that couldn't have happened."

"Why would anyone do that?"

"For obvious reasons. They now claim that there is no more gold in the mine. I don't know how much they have taken out, but they have certainly sold it. So they want that money plus the two million dollars from us. It should add up to a tidy sum."

She frowned. "But how can you keep them from collecting from your company?"

"All I have to do is to prove that they knew exactly how little gold there was in the mine, so all they had to do was make sure that we'd go for the report and give them the insurance. Which we did."

"But Mr. Smith—"

"I know," I interrupted. "We already went over that. He could have made an honest error. Or someone could have tampered with the report in some way before or after it was written."

"I don't know much about insurance," she said, "but I would think an insurance company wouldn't sell a policy like that."

"Most of them don't. We do. Of course, we charge an extra heavy premium for such policies, so we make more money than on a regular policy—if we don't slip up."

"Well, I hope you find what you're looking for. But how are you going to prove anything?"

"I have my own system," I said with a smile. "Oh, I'll do some looking around. Probably this afternoon. I know pretty much who is involved, and then I start pushing them a little, letting them know that I know something but not how much. People get nervous, and then frightened, when they're exposed to that. When they are nervous or frightened, they start making mistakes. Then all I have to do is stand around and watch for the mistakes. After that, it's only a matter of time."

"I don't understand," she said. There was a frown on her face, and she looked like she was nervous. She probably was.

I lit a fresh cigarette and glanced at my watch. "I think it must be time for you to get back to the office. And for me to get to work."

"I thought you never worked."

"I'll tell you a little secret, honey, but don't tell anyone else. The truth is that when I'm on a case, I never stop working."

"You confuse me, Milo. Half of the time I don't understand what you're saying." Now she did sound nervous. "What are you going to do this afternoon?"

"I'm going to find out more about gold. I might even become an expert on it. I may have to become an alchemist and prepare a philosopher's stone."

"What's a philosopher's stone?"

"A legendary substance that was believed capable of transforming base metals like lead into precious gold and silver. Legions of medieval alchemists—from mystics and magicians to emperors and popes—tried to discover the recipe for the stone, but there is no evidence that anyone succeeded. Charles the Second of England had an alchemical laboratory built beneath the royal bedchamber, with a secret staircase leading to it. It never produced anything either—except, perhaps, moments of pleasure for royal chamberlains with a penchant for voyeurism."

"Voyeurism?" she asked.

"Watching or listening to a man and a maid engaged in the oldest sport in the world—making 'the beast with two backs,' as they called it. A fifteenth-century alchemist called Bernard of Trèves thought he had finally discovered the perfect recipe for making gold. He mixed two thousand egg yolks with olive oil and vitriol, and cooked it on a slow fire for two weeks. But all he accomplished was poisoning his pigs when he finally gave up and fed it to them."

"Do you make all these things up?"

"No, my dear. Occasionally, between drinks, I read a book. You might also be interested to know that when the United States finally declared throughout the world that thirteen and five-sevenths grains of gold would henceforth be worth one dollar, the natives of the Solomon Islands didn't give a damn. They knew that five hundred dolphin teeth would buy a good wife. That put them ahead of the game."*

"How on earth is all that junk going to help you solve the case?" she wanted to know.

"I haven't the faintest idea. Maybe the only thing that will come out of it is a bad epigram. Like: All is not gold that jitters."

"Good-bye, Milo," she said as we left the Waldorf. "Thank you for the lovely lunch—and our unusual conversation. Will I see you again?"

"Why not? I'll be around for a while."

She took a few steps, then stopped and turned around. "Can you be serious long enough to tell me what you're looking for?"

---

* In 1934, the Gold Reserve Act, signed by President Franklin Delano Roosevelt, transferred ownership of all monetary gold in the country to the U.S. Treasury, and the price was set at $35 a fine ounce, equivalent to 13 5/7 (13.71) grains. As for dolphin teeth, Solomon Islanders still use this form of currency (including as a bride price), killing more than a thousand dolphins a year, despite the efforts of environmentalists to stop the practice.

"Sure. The answer to a very simple question. How can one take gold ore out of a mine that very possibly has no gold in it?"

She shook her head and turned away. I watched her walk down the street. It should have given me pleasure, but my head was too filled with questions about gold. I turned and went my own way.

I stopped at the drugstore and looked in the Yellow Pages of the phone book. I found the name of a gold broker on Commercial Row. The address wasn't far away, so I walked to it. On the outside, it looked like an old hock shop. In fact, it was. At least partly. The sign on the window announced that the shop also bought and sold old gold. Then a small, more faded sign added that there was a gold broker on the premises.

I opened the door and walked in. There was nobody in sight until finally a man appeared from the back. He looked me over quickly, as though checking to see if I had something to pawn. He was well past middle age and was well dressed. He lifted his gaze to my face. There was an expression in his eyes that seemed to say that he'd seen everything and there were no more surprises.

"May I help you?" he asked mildly.

"I hope so," I said. "Do you buy gold?"

"Old gold?"

I shook my head. "New gold."

The expression in his eyes changed. "You have a mine around here?"

"No."

His eyes changed again. "Hot gold?" he asked wearily.

"No. I want some information." For the first time, he looked surprised.

"Cop?" he asked. "If you were a local cop you'd know that I have a license to buy and sell gold. If you're not a local cop, what's the beef?"

"No cop and no beef. I represent an insurance company in New York." I showed him my card. "All I want is some information."

"What about?"

"There's a gold mine up in the hills called the Natural Gold Mine?"

"Anybody in town could have told you that."

"Anybody in town wouldn't have a license to buy gold and might just be repeating some gossip he'd heard."

He nodded. "That's about the size of it. What's an insurance company's interest in it?"

"We issued a policy covering the mine, mostly based on an assay report we received. It covered the possible producing life of the mine. Now they have put in a claim for the face value of the policy, and there are strong indications that the value of the mine was greatly exaggerated. Do you know the men who own the mine?"

"I know one of them by reputation, which does not make him out to be a pillar of society. I know one of them only as a name. And I know one of them only from seeing him when he's bringing in gold. His name is Jerry Lake. He never did amount to much, and he got into trouble a few times, though nothing serious. He was working as shotgun for a while at the Palomino Mare, which is owned by Dino Mancetti, the senior member of the mining company. I guess he got promoted."

"A local boy?"

"Yes, but he's a little older than a boy by now."

"The others local too?" I asked.

"Well, not exactly. Mancetti came here about ten years ago. Don't know where he's from. He has three or four businesses, all of them legal, even the Mare, which is frowned on by the church ladies in town, but they can't do anything about it."

"Why not?"

"It's in another county. It's legal there."

"What about the third man?"

"Nick Lancer. I've never seen him and don't know where he's from. I hear he don't hang around in town very much."

"Probably playing it smart," I said. "Can you tell me how much gold they've sold to you since the mine was opened?"

"I can tell you exactly if you give me a minute," he said. He walked to the rear of the store and went through a door. From the brief glimpse I got, it appeared to be an office. He was gone for only a couple of minutes, then returned with a ledger book. He started turning the pages.

"Here it is," he said finally. "Well, it's a little less than a ton of gold. That's not gold ore, you understand, but just gold molded into bricks."

"Any stamp on the bricks?"

He nodded. "Each brick is stamped with a pair of dice. The total of the spots showing is seven."

"A natural. Is it high-grade gold?"

"More than ninety-nine percent. You can't ask for any better."

"Any idea how much it's worth?"

"Not exactly. When Lake brought in a delivery the other day, he said there'll be one more delivery in—let's see—two days from now, and that would be the last. That should bring it up to a ton, and that should be worth more than one million dollars."

"More than one million?" I said. "I thought there was supposed to be millions of dollars there. The assay report made it sound like it, too."

"Easy to make it sound like it," he said with a smile. "Not so easy to dig it out. That would be nothing in a really big mine with the modern machinery, but it's pretty good for a little mine—especially one that has been abandoned as being empty for the last hundred years."

"I guess so," I admitted. "How do you suppose that everyone believed there was no gold in the mine for a hundred years, and then suddenly there is gold?"

"I think most people would call it luck."

"I have an idea," I said dryly, "that the present owners of this gold mine are more apt to be percentage players. By the way, you forgot to tell me your name."

"You forgot to ask. It's William Poe. It says so right on the window. Nobody ever sees anything except 'Gold Broker.' "

"Any relation to John Poe of Poeville?" I asked.

"Distantly," he said, "but not near enough to inherit anything from the Poe mine, if there was anything to inherit. Although I suppose I do owe one thing to the connection.

An ancestor of mine started dealing in gold about that time. And there's always been somebody in every generation of my family who had something to do with gold. Not digging it, though. You seem to have been doing your homework on gold mines."

"Some, but I haven't learned enough to make me the hit of a party. It only makes me feel like the man who was at a party where everyone was passionately engaged in conversation on some learned subject and leaving him out of it. But he has one little nugget of information, which he was saving for an opening that never came. So, as soon as someone stopped to take a deep breath, he dropped his nugget. But it turned out to be a conversation stopper instead of a starter."

"What was that?"

"Did you know that dinosaurs had no scrotums?"

He laughed. "Can't say that I did. Is it true?"

"I never bothered to find out. Proof would not enhance it, but would only damage its beauty. There is one more thing I'd like to know, but I don't think it has anything to do with my case. Do you know Homer Ambrose Fenner?"

"Sure. And Necktie, too. They're practically landmarks around here. You met them?"

I nodded. "They took me up to see their mine yesterday."

"Well, Ambrose must have taken a fancy to you if he brought you up there. He's never been closemouthed about his mine, but I don't know anybody he's ever invited up to see it. And he never brags about it. The story is that he won the mine in a poker game, maybe forty years ago. He never looked in it to see if there was any gold until just a few years ago. I guess it wasn't easy for him to get a job, and not having anything else to do, he went up and poked around and found some gold. Necktie was never anything more than a handyman, but it was getting harder for him to get a job, so Ambrose invited him to live in the rickety old house he owned, and they've been living together and working the mine together ever since then."

"You buy their gold? They told me they take enough out of it to get by on."

"That's about it. They bring their gold in maybe once a month. They don't work too hard, and they get enough money to pay taxes and utilities, buy their food, clothes, and bourbon. I guess that's all they want."

"Sounds like enough," I agreed. "I'm curious about one thing. The Natural Gold Mine is right next to their mine. Could the men working it have managed to tap Ambrose's vein and might that be where their gold is coming from?"

"From the way Ambrose describes his vein, I don't think it's possible for them to get as much gold out of it as they've sold. There is one other thing peculiar about them and their mine. I don't know the answer to it, but you might keep it in mind."

"What's that?"

"Not one of those three knows anything about mining, and I doubt if even one of them ever did a day of honest, hard work in his life."

"I have the same feeling about them. But where and how did they get the gold they've been selling you?"

"I don't know," he said. "I've wondered about it. But they're bringing the gold out. Somebody had to dig out the ore, separate the gold from the rocks, and mold it into bricks. And that's hard work. If they had hired anyone else, Ambrose would've seen them entering or leaving the mine."

"I guess so. Well ... thanks, Mr. Poe."

"Not at all, Mr. March. I was glad to have some company. Drop in anytime."

I nodded and walked to the door and turned to look back at him. "You have a license to buy and sell gold, Mr. Poe. When you buy gold, as you have been doing from the Natural Gold Mine, where do you sell it?"

"It's true," he said with a smile, "that Reno is not an actual thriving gold center and I can only sell to persons who have a license to buy, and then it will depend upon the amount of gold their license will permit them to buy. I can sell to them and make a small profit. They can do the same thing. But believe me, nobody gets rich from the available gold. I sell most of what I do get to brokers in San Francisco. I can assure you that they adhere strictly to the guidelines set by their license."

"I didn't doubt that. I just wondered how it was done. Thanks again."

I opened the door and went out. I walked to Virginia Street and stopped there, thinking about it. A freight train was going by, and it gave me an idea. It wasn't much of an idea, but it was all I had at the moment. I walked up to the train station. It looked as if it had seen better days.

It looked pretty much the same way inside. I finally saw a window with a man sitting behind it. He looked like he was glad to see someone walk in.

"Are you the freight agent?" I asked.

He nodded.

"Doesn't look like you're overwhelmed with business."

"Not exactly," he said. "You new in town?"

"Sort of. I'm from New York City."

"Aiming to bring freight in here or send it out?"

"Neither. I'm looking for information."

"We don't give out much information," he said, "unless it's for people aiming to ship with us. What's your business?"

"Insurance. I'm here looking into a case where we believe there may have been fraud. The product involved may have been shipped from here by rail. Have you had any gold shipments during the past year?"

"We don't get many shipments of gold from here. Haven't for years."

"I didn't ask you that," I said. "I did ask if you had any shipments during the past year. That includes even one shipment. And if you have, then I want to know who made one shipment or more."

He gave me a mirthless grin. "I told you we don't give out much information."

"If you want to play it the hard way, I can go downtown and get a court order for your appearance with the records, and some reliable member of your company will also have to appear. It may take a day or two, but I can do it. If you'd rather make it easier on yourself, we can handle it another way. It's up to you."

"What's the other way?" he asked.

"What's your name?"

"Clem Blatchik. Why?"

"Do you accept shipments of gold? Say, from here to San Francisco?"

"If somebody wants to ship some, we do. That is, if it's legal. How big a load?"

I took my watch from my left wrist and put it on the counter in front of him. You didn't have to be a jeweler to see that it was an expensive watch. "I never had it weighed, but this is what I want sent."

"By freight?" he asked incredulously. "It ain't even packed."

"I didn't have time to pack it," I said gravely. "Of course, I will pay for any packing costs and any other fees involved in the transference of the shipment. This should cover it." I put a hundred dollar bill on the counter.

"Well, it's highly irregular, but—" He reached for the money. "Where do you want it sent?"

"Just a minute," I said, putting my hand on the bill. "That watch is gold. Before I turn it over to you, I want to know if you have had any recent experience with shipments of gold, no matter how small they are."

I could see he was beginning to get the idea. "Where do you want it sent?"

"I was thinking of giving it to the Salvation Army in San Francisco. I'll tell you what I'll do. You transfer it to any charity that you think is a worthy one, and that will be fine with me. But first I'd like to hear about your shipments of gold."

His face was full of understanding. "I reckon that's proper," he said. "We've made several shipments of gold from Reno in the last several months. I'd say between ten and twenty shipments. All of them were small, and they must have been delivered all right."

"Who made the shipments?"

"All by one company."

"What's the name of the company?"

"The New Yukon Mining Corporation."

"A Reno company?"

He shook his head. His eyes were fixed on the hundred dollars I was still holding down. "Nope. They got offices in Carson City."

"Who are the owners?"

"I don't know. I've only seen one man, and I guess he just works for them. He delivers every load and signs all the papers. His name is Nacker. Albert Nacker. He ain't from Reno, I'm sure, but I never asked him where he was from."

"Where'd they ship the gold to?"

"Some gold broker in San Francisco. Guess that's the nearest place to find a big broker."

"What do you think the value of the gold they shipped would come to?"

"No idea. All I know is that they've insured every shipment and the total insurance adds up to the neighborhood of two million dollars. I wouldn't mind having that myself."

"It's a good neighborhood," I agreed. "Do you know where their mine is?"

"No. I asked a few times but I didn't get a straight answer. It must not be too far away or they wouldn't be shipping from here."

"Maybe. Maybe not. All right, you can take care of the watch." I took my hand off the bill and started to turn away.

"Just a minute," he said. "What's your name?"

"Milo March."

"How do I know that's your name?"

I took out my identification and showed it to him. "And that's the company I work for."

"I guess it's all right. But how do I know that you won't wait a few days and then claim I stole it from you?"

"You don't," I admitted, "but you have my word for it. If I happen to find out that you've told anyone about our conversation today, I might change my mind. I also have the number on that bill. Think that over. Thanks."

He muttered something under his breath as I left. I walked to Virginia Street, thinking about our conversation. I doubted if I had learned anything that would be useful to me, but I'd still check out the corporation in Carson City and find out who the owners were.

I decided I was tired and that I would go back to the hotel. There was something I wanted to do that night and I hadn't had much sleep the night before. I went straight to the LTD and drove back to the hotel. As I entered, I noticed there was something in my box. I asked for it and the girl handed it to me.

It was a telephone message. It wasn't very informative. It merely said that a man had phoned, said that he'd heard I hadn't kept my reservation to New York and that he hoped I'd remember to keep my reservation for the following morning. There was no name on it. I called the girl over and showed her the message.

"Were you here when this was received?" I asked.

"Yes, Mr. March. I didn't know that you were checking out tomorrow morning."

"I'm not. Didn't the man leave his name?"

"No. I asked him for his name, but he said you'd know who it was."

"Okay. I've had a rough day, so I'm going upstairs to have a nap. I'd like to be called at five o'clock. And if that same man calls again, put him through to me. I'll give him my opinion of people who play practical jokes and think it's great fun."

"All right, Mr. March." There was a slightly worried look on her face. "Is everything all right, Mr. March?"

"Everything is just peachy," I said.

I stopped to pick up a paper and then, not wanting the bellman to come up when he felt like it, I got my own bucket of ice and went upstairs. I hung up my jacket and made myself a drink. I opened the paper and browsed through it while I had my drink. When it was finished, I kicked off my shoes and stretched out on the bed. I was asleep almost as soon as my head was on the pillow.

SEVEN

The noise was as loud as a three-alarm fire. One that kept repeating. Finally I got the message. The telephone was ringing. I swung my feet to the floor and picked up the receiver.

"Hold it a minute," I said, and put the receiver down on the small desk. I felt my way across the room, found a glass, splashed some gin and orange juice in it, and threw in an ice cube. I took one good swallow and I was awake enough to make the return trip. On the way, I glanced at my watch, only to remember I didn't have one anymore.

I sat down on the edge of the bed and lit a cigarette. Then I picked up the receiver.

"Yeah?" I said.

"March?" he said. It was the same voice I'd heard the night before.

"Hello, Nick," I said. "What's wrong? Don't you have any private life, so you have to go to a phone and make anonymous calls? Is that your thing?"

"Go to hell. Are you catching that plane in the morning?"

"Now that you mention it, I don't think I will. I haven't quite finished what I came here to do. Besides, it might rob some poor guy of a seat and he would miss getting to New York in time to see his poor, sick old mother before she died.

I'd never forgive myself. Now, what's on what we laughingly call your mind?"

He said a short four-letter word, followed by a three-letter word. It suggested an unattractive possibility, which I ignored. "Remember when I called yesterday? I mentioned a man you met in Florida."

"You mean Angelo Bacci."

"I didn't say no name. He wants to see you."

"In Florida?"

"Here in Reno. He's staying at Harrah's. In a suite. He's calling himself Joseph Bottelli. He wants to see you tonight at about six. He said to tell you it will be a friendly meeting."

"He must be losing his grip," I said. "You mean he's inviting me to a friendly chat over cocktails?"

"He only said he wanted you to be there. What'll I tell him?"

"If anything comes up that's more interesting, I won't be there. If nothing does come up and I'm bored, I might drop in for a few laughs. Why don't you tell him that, and then go somewhere and play dead?" I put the receiver down on the phone and thought for a minute. It must be earlier than five o'clock. I had asked to be called. I picked up the phone again and dialed the operator.

"This is Mr. March," I said when she answered. "I'm awake, so you may cancel the call I left."

I put the phone down again and lit a cigarette. I sipped at my drink. Angelo Bacci wanted to see me. He was in Reno, under a phony name. There hadn't been any mention of him in the papers. He was well enough known in the Syndicate to have been spotted by someone who would have called the papers. Why did he want to see me?

That was a good question. I wasn't working on anything connected with the Syndicate. Or was I? I remembered having heard that Dino Mancetti was a minor member of the Mob. Why was he important enough to bring a capo like Bacci all the way from Florida to help him? So far as I was concerned, Mancetti hadn't committed any crime except fraud against an insurance company. They couldn't send out a couple of hoods to scare Intercontinental into buttoning their collective lip.

There was only one way to find out. See Bacci. I snuffed out my cigarette, finished the drink, got undressed, and went into the bathroom. I shaved and showered, and by the time I was dressed I felt as good as if I'd had a full night of sleep.

I drove downtown in the LTD and put it in the parking lot on Sierra. I walked up the alley to Second Street, then down to Virginia. On the way, I stopped in a jewelry store and bought the most expensive watch they had. It could go on the expense account as a replacement for the watch and hundred dollars I'd left at the depot. I set the watch and noticed it was ten minutes to six.

There was no point in standing on the street watching the stampede of tourists on their way to the casinos. I walked on to Harrah's and up to the desk.

"Yes, sir?" It was the clerk.

"Mr. Bottelli?"

"Are you expected, sir?"

"I don't know if I'm expected," I said, "but I was invited."

"Who shall I say is calling, sir?"

"Milo March."

He turned to the phone and talked briefly, although I couldn't hear what he was saying. There was a smile on his face as he came back to me.

"Mr. Bottelli is expecting you, Mr. March. He has suites one and two on the top floor."

I thanked him and walked over to the bank of elevators. As I waited, I was thinking about the security measures that seemed to exist for Mr. Bacci's safety. Then I realized I was getting paranoid. If the hotel had known who he was, someone in the hotel would have tipped off the newspapers. So all they knew was that there was a Mr. Bottelli who was obviously very rich and wanted privacy, and all the management was doing was giving him the degree of privacy he wanted.

The elevator came and I told the operator I wanted the top floor. He nodded, so I guessed that the desk had called and told him it was all right to take me up. He didn't wait for other passengers but took me right up.

There were two doors fairly near the elevator. I guessed that the first was number 1 and the second number 2. Naturally, Bacci would have to be number 1 and the other would be for his guards. I stepped over to it and pressed the buzzer. The door opened a couple of inches.

"You March?" a voice asked.

"Yes."

"It's March," the same voice bellowed.

"Let the bum in." It sounded like Bacci.

The door swung open and I stepped inside. It was a large

room, filled with comfortable furniture and a bar. There were three men there. The one who had let me in was a typical-looking hood. He wasn't wearing a jacket, and his gun and holster were in plain view. I vaguely remembered him before. The other was slightly younger, but he looked just as tough. He, too, carried a gun under his left arm. He was leaning against the bar, staring at me with the blank expression of a merchant looking for a cheap buy. I'd never seen him either, but I did know the third man.

Angelo Bacci. In his late forties. He wore expensive, well-fitted clothes. He was short and his body was barrel-like, but I knew that it was all muscle, no fat. He was holding a drink in one hand. There was a smile on his face, but there was no humor in it.

"Hello, Milo," he said. "Sit down and have a drink."

"Hello, Angelo," I said. I moved over to a chair which was placed so I could watch all of them. "Since everyone isn't formal, is it all right if I take off my jacket?"

"Sure, Milo. Make yourself at home."

I took off my jacket and tossed it over the back of the chair, then sat down. I could see the other two men looking at my gun.

"Makes it more comfortable for everyone," I said pleasantly. "Now anyone can grab for his gun without worrying about catching it on his jacket when he pulls it."

"They ain't going to do no shooting unless it's necessary," Bacci said, grinning. "I wouldn't want them to put any holes in the furniture. This is a classy hotel, and I wouldn't want they should think I wasn't good enough to stay here."

"Perish the thought," I said. "I'll have that drink now. If your boy knows how to make a dry martini, I'll have one. But tell him to go very light on the chloral hydrate.* I'm allergic to it."

He leaned back his head and laughed. "You were always a card, Milo. If I didn't hate you so much, I'd like you. And I'll still give you a job if you want it."

"The hours are too long." I waited until the young gunman brought over my drink and plunked it down in front of me. Some of it splashed over onto the coffee table. "Your bartender's a little careless."

"It ain't his regular trade," he said. He thought that was a great joke, too.

"I would never have guessed. I thought that thing under his left arm was a swizzle stick." I lifted my glass. "Well, here's to crime."

"You remember Hackett, don't you?" he asked.

"Vaguely. He was a part of your zoo in Miami Beach, wasn't he? How is he?"

"Dead," he said flatly. "He never got over the bullets you put in him.** It was probably just as well. The bulls were trying to get a deathbed confession out of him. He might have talked too much."

"And Ketcher?"

"He didn't die, but his leg ain't been much good since then.

---

* Adding chloral hydrate would make the drink a "Mickey Finn" (chloral hydrate now also has a reputation as a date rape drug). Milo has never been slipped a Mickey in any of the books, although in *The Splintered Man* he was forced to take LSD.
** Milo shot Dan Hackett in *The Bonded Dead*.

I sort of retired him after he got out of the can. He only had to do one and a half, and then I got him sprung."

"Fringe benefits, too," I murmured. "What about Daly and Dixon?"

"Somebody shot Dixon," he said, shaking his head. "It shook Daly up so much that he changed his plea to guilty and admitted it was another night that he was playing cards with me. He'd put up them two girls to lifting the bonds and then he killed one of them. But I proved that I'd only seen him that one night and I didn't know anything about them bonds, and I came out of it clean."

"That's nice."

"Give Milo another martini, Jack," Bacci ordered. He waited until the order was carried out. He gestured toward the other gunman, who was still standing by the door. "Did you take a good look at Tony when you came in?" Bacci asked me.

"No. Why should I?"

"No special reason. I thought you might remember that he was a good friend of Hackett's. He's still a little upset about it. Of course, he won't do nothing as long as I tell him not to."

"I'm glad to hear he's well trained." I lit a cigarette. "How come you're here under a phony name?"

"Ah," he grunted. "I don't like all that publicity. It's bad for business. I just felt like a little vacation. Then, I've got some interests here, too. How about you, Milo?"

"Business."

"I hear you're interested in gold."

"Isn't everyone?"

"Yeah, I guess. I got a friend here who's got something going for him in a gold mine. I hear you might be pushing him around a little."

"Dino?" It had already occurred to me that there might be some connection.

"Yeah. Dino's an old friend of mine. Like a younger brother, you might say. I hear you been pushing him."

"Not yet," I said evenly, "but I've been thinking about it. He's trying to pull something on my company. I'm just here to see that he doesn't get too enthusiastic about it."

"I wouldn't like it if you was to push him."

"That's too bad," I said. "If you're such a good friend of his, why don't you just send your two Rover boys down to spend money at his Palomino Mare and stay out of everything else?"

"They don't like his joint. There's another one not much farther away they like better. They say it has a better class of broads."

"Well, if that indicates how fond you are of Dino, you might relax and tell me the real story about Dino's gold mine."

"What real story? He and two other boys bought a gold mine and found it had quite a bit of gold. They've been mining it themselves and selling it. A perfectly legitimate business."

"If it's so legitimate, why are they supposed to be doing all the work? I doubt if Dino ever did any work harder than running a whorehouse. And that punk I saw in front of the mine with a shotgun looked as if the only way he ever got a callus was by pulling a trigger. The whole thing's a laugh. Even the assay report he got."

"It's legitimate," he said stubbornly. "I'm just trying to help you, Milo. I'd hate to see you get hurt."

"I'm deeply touched," I said dryly. I stood up. "I gather that's all you wanted to see me about, and I have a busy evening ahead of me. Thanks for the drinks, Angelo. Are you going to be around town long?"

"I'm not sure," he said glumly. "I have to take care of my business. Maybe I can see you again before I go. You won't forget what I said?"

"How could I forget anything you said, Angelo?" I put on my jacket and walked across the room. Tony was still standing in front of the door. I stopped and looked at him.

"Do you want to step to one side?" I asked. "Or would you rather have me help you?"

He hesitated a minute and then stepped aside, but his face was tight with anger.

"I'll be seeing you around, March," he said.

"Sure, you will, baby. Just make certain that you see me quick enough. I can't stand shooting people who don't know what is happening." I took a step nearer the door and shifted slightly to look at him. "Hold out your hand," I said pleasantly.

He was concentrating on staring at me, but he automatically put out his hand. I reached over and dropped my cigarette into it. "Hold that for me until I get back," I said. I opened the door and stepped outside. I walked toward the elevator.

"Tony!" I heard Bacci bellow. There was a moment of silence, then the door was slammed shut so hard I thought it must have splintered. Without looking back, I went over to the elevator and pushed the button.

The elevator arrived. As the door opened, I could hear a

voice shouting from the other side of the door to the suite. I stepped into the elevator and we started down. I noticed that the operator was staring at me.

"What's going on in there?" he asked.

"Sounded like someone arguing. It's not surprising. They're rather crude people."

"You know them guys?"

"I know one of them, but he's not exactly a bosom pal. I had a strange feeling they didn't like me very much."

He was shaking his head as I left the elevator. Out on the street, I looked at my watch. It was still early, so I could have a leisurely dinner and still have plenty of time to reach the house where I wanted to go. I walked up to the Waldorf.

I had a drink at the bar with Joe and cut up some old touches. Then I told him to mix another one and send it back to me. I went back to a table and told the girl I had a martini coming. When she brought it, I ordered dinner.

By the time I finished dinner, I decided it was time to go. I paid the check and started out, but I saw that Joe had remembered something and already had a glass of brandy waiting for me on the bar. I stopped and had it and talked with him some more. Then I left for the parking lot where I'd put the LTD.

I didn't remember the name of the street where Ambrose and Necktie lived, but I was certain that I knew how to find it. I stopped on the way and bought a bottle of bourbon. I also had enough foresight to buy a few paper cups and then drove on to the house. There was no light inside the house, so it probably meant they weren't home yet. I parked in front and relaxed. After a while I opened the bottle and poured myself a small shot of the bourbon, lit a cigarette, and went back to relaxing.

I heard the old truck sometime before it arrived. Finally it was there and pulled in beside the house. I knew they would be wondering about the car in front of their house. I finished the bourbon in the paper cup and got out and walked slowly toward the truck.

"Hello, Ambrose, Necktie," I said.

"It's Milo," Ambrose said. Then he raised his voice slightly. "It was too dark to see who it was. Thought it might be some-body aiming to ambush us."

"Who would do a thing like that?" I asked. I stopped beside the truck.

"You never can tell," Necktie said, climbing out of the truck. "There's a lot of ornery coyotes around. Course, I don't have to worry none as long as they ain't carrying a rope."

Ambrose was already down on the ground and started moving toward the house. "Wasn't expecting to see you tonight, Milo," he said. "Come on in and set a spell. If you can find a place to set. Necktie ain't very good at doing his chores."

"A man ain't supposed to do a woman's work. Ain't right."

Ambrose chuckled as he opened the door and turned on a light. We all trooped inside. "You're welcome to set down and have some vittles with us as soon as Necktie stops gabbing and rustles them up."

"Danged old fool acts like I was a hired hand," Necktie grumbled.

"No, thanks. I ate while I was downtown. But I did think

that all that mining today might have made your throats dry, so I brought along some gargle for you." I put the bottle on the table.

"Now, that Milo's right neighborly," Necktie said. "A fellow don't mind going out and getting some clean glasses when he comes. Course, we don't rightly need it. There's still plenty left in that big jug you fetched in last night."

"You talk more'n a danged woman, Necktie. Get movin'. Maybe the man's thirsty."

Necktie grumbled again under his breath but disappeared into the kitchen. Ambrose took off his hat and threw it into the corner of the room. Then he dropped into a chair. "Set, Milo. Necktie'll be right in with the glasses. He's a good boy, but he just ain't ever been on very good talking terms with work."

I sat in a chair and lit a cigarette. "Have a good day?"

"About like always. We dug out about as much as we always do. It's enough. Both of us is getting too old for more work than that. How was your day, Milo?"

"Not bad. I think I may have struck a few veins of gold myself. They might pan out pretty good if I just keep digging."

Necktie came in with the glasses. He'd even managed to come up with some ice cubes. There was something about the sight of a bottle that made Necktie expand.

"What kind of digging?" he asked.

"A little like yours. The only difference is that I dig at people instead of rocks. Sometimes it pays off just as well. There's also a lot of fool's gold that turns up."

"You think you can prove them guys in the mine next to us are crooks?" Necktie wanted to know.

"I think I can—but I'll be damned if I know how. Did either of you ever hear of the New Yukon Mining Corporation?"

They both shook their heads. "That's a new one on me," Ambrose said. "Where's their mine?"

"I don't know. It's a new corporation, and they have their office in Carson City. And they're producing gold which they're selling in San Francisco. It's probably a coincidence that there are two old mines that opened about the same time, and both are producing gold. But I don't believe in coincidences. Are you planning on working tomorrow?"

"I reckon," Ambrose said. "Our grubstake's getting a little low, and I figured we'd work steady for the next two or three days. Why?"

"I want to hire you for a couple of days." I pulled out some money and stripped off two hundred dollars and placed the bills on the table. "That should take care of what you'll lose by working for me. If it's not enough, say so and I'll fatten the pot."

"That's too much," Ambrose said. "If you need some help, we'll give it to you. We don't want to take your money, Milo."

"It's not my money. It belongs to the company I work for. They pay my expenses in addition to my salary. You'll be part of my expenses."

"Well … ," Ambrose said uncertainly.

"Take it," I said. "If you do what I ask, you won't be able to work the mine tomorrow or the following day. You'll have to sleep sometime."

Ambrose picked up the money, divided it into two parts, and handed one to Necktie. "What do you want us to do, Milo?"

"I want to go up to your mine again tomorrow night. What time do those men next door knock off and leave?"

"Don't rightly know," Ambrose said. "They used to leave about the same time we did, but lately they been staying later. I guess maybe they do their molding at night and then load up their truck and leave. What you got in mind?"

"I'll bet I know what he's got in mind," Necktie said excitedly. "The same thing I got in mind. He wants to see inside that place."

"That's more or less it, Necktie," I said. "I do want to see inside. That's the only way I can get one piece of information that I need."

"I know just the way you can get in, too," Necktie said. "I'll bet anything there is a hole between the two mines. Where those shrubs are growing. I'll bet we can get through easy as anything."

"You're a danged old fool," Ambrose said. "Almost any old mine has them shrubs growing out of the rocks. Don't mean a thing. Look at the things that grow in the desert. At least the things that grow in the mines get water."

"Don't worry about it," I said. "Once they are gone, I can get into it from the front."

"What's your idea, Milo?" Ambrose said. "We don't know exactly when they'll knock it off and go home."

"What about the shotgun? Does he stay out there all the time?"

"Don't think so. They were loading up their truck a couple of times when we left and all three of them was doing it."

"I thought," I said, "we might go up there about ten o'clock at night. If they've already left, we'll just go up and do what we want to. If they're still there, we can leave our car somewhere down the hill and walk up quietly and go into your mine without making any noise. Then we stay in there quietly until we hear them leave. What do you think?"

"Might work," he said. "We could hide that jeep you got back of them big bushes along the road. They wouldn't see it as they left. We could walk up quiet-like and get into my mine without them knowing it. We could keep quiet then, just in case Necktie has stumbled on something with that crazy idea of his."

"I'm telling you … ," Necktie started eagerly. That was as far as he got.

"You already told us more'n you know," Ambrose said. "To be safe, we're going to act as if we believe you even though we don't. Sound all right, Milo?"

"Sounds good to me. Let's have a drink on it and then I'll take off and I'll see you tomorrow night."

Necktie poured three drinks and brought some more ice from the kitchen. His face showed that he was so excited he could hardly keep his mouth shut, but the expression on Ambrose's face was enough to keep him quiet. I downed my drink and stood up.

"I'll pick you up tomorrow night."

"What time?" Ambrose asked.

"About the same time as I came tonight," I said. "That'll give you plenty of time to have your supper and we should get there about the right time."

Ambrose nodded. "We'll be waiting for you."

"You bet we will," Necktie said. "Ambrose will see that I'm right when we get in there and see the vein they been working on and—"

"That ain't why we're going," Ambrose interrupted. "Good night, Milo."

"Good night," I said, smiling. "See you tomorrow night." I went out and drove away.

I went straight back to the hotel. I had to wait for the oncoming traffic before I could make a left turn into the parking lot. I happened to glance to my right where there was a car parked. There was nothing unusual about that, but there was a man sitting behind the wheel smoking a cigarette. He took a drag on the cigarette and I got a faint glimpse of his face. There was something familiar about it, but I couldn't place him at once.

The last car passed and I made the left turn into the lot. I was still thinking of the face I had glimpsed as I drove along looking for a place to park. Then it hit me. The man in the car had been Tony Roma, Bacci's gunman who had stayed by the door all the time I was in the suite. There was no chance that he was parked by my hotel by accident, and I doubted he was there because he wanted a quiet conversation with me.

There was a parking place next to my jeep. I swung into it and cut the motor. I glanced out the window. The car was still parked on the street, and he hadn't gotten out of it. I doubted if he would follow me into the hotel, because that would be too dangerous. If I walked over to the entrance, he might try to get me then, but I doubted he would. It would be a long and difficult shot, and he would have only the one shot. He might hope that I wouldn't stay long at the hotel. Then he could follow me until he had a good chance.

I climbed out of the LTD and into the jeep. I backed out and drove past the hotel, turning south on the adjoining street. Looking in the rearview mirror, I saw him start up and drive straight ahead. I drove slowly, making it easy for him. As I guessed, he turned left at the next block, then swung in behind me. I went ahead at a very moderate speed, still making it easy for him. He followed at about the same speed.

Now it was up to me. I remembered a spot that I thought would help me find out if he merely wanted to see where I went or was more interested in seeing that I didn't go anywhere.

We finally reached a fairly quiet part of the street. Ahead was Virginia Lake, where the street split into two parts. One swung to the left while the other swung around to the right, running through a quiet residential section. I took that one. There was practically no traffic on it. As he followed, I took my gun from the holster and flicked off the safety catch, then put it in my lap.

We rounded a curve, and ahead there was a fairly straight stretch of street with no other cars in sight. A glance in the mirror showed that he was speeding up.

I slackened my speed just slightly, picked up my gun, and waited.

EIGHT

He had swung to the left and was going to pass me. I took my foot from the accelerator, holding the wheel with my left hand, and raised the gun slightly.

As he crept up even with me, I could see that he'd rolled down his window and was raising his gun. I ignored everything else and concentrated on lining my gun up. When it was in the right position, I squeezed the trigger gently. I saw his head jerk to one side. I dropped my gun in my lap and hit the brakes as hard as I could. His car slid past me and at the same time I heard a bullet making a thin sound over my head.

His car careened to one side and ran into a tree. I took a quick check. There were no cars in either direction. I swung the jeep around and drove back the way I had come and took a right turn. I drove fairly fast for two blocks, then switched to another street. I made three more turns and ended up on Virginia Street. I slowed down, slipped my gun back in the holster, and drove carefully back toward the hotel. Somewhere in the distance there was the keening cry of a siren.

It was a short drive to the hotel. I parked next to the LTD and went in. There was a message in my box, but it only said that someone had called and left no name. I stopped and picked up a carton of cigarettes and the evening paper, got a bucket of ice, and went up to my room.

I was good and tired. It had been a long day, and the next day would be even longer. I hung up my jacket, kicked off my shoes, and made a drink of gin and orange juice. I went through the paper slowly, but there wasn't anything of interest to me. Finally, I got undressed and went to sleep.

I was up early the next morning. I shaved and showered and phoned room service for breakfast. It wasn't long before there was the rap on the door. The waiter was obviously still enlarging the plans for his house. He put my breakfast on the table, added the carefully folded morning paper, and then put a yellow envelope in front of me.

"There was a telegram for you, sir," he said. "I took the liberty of bringing it up to you."

"Thank you," I said. I took the check, added a tip that was sure to bring a smile to his face, and signed it. He escorted his smile out of the room.

I ripped open the telegram and spread it out. It wasn't, as I expected, from New York. I read it:

will arrive in los angeles the morning after you receive this. will rest there for a couple of hours then drive to reno. should be there in time for us to have dinner together. love mei.

I had been so immersed in my own little puzzle, I had almost forgotten that she was coming. It was good news. I wondered idly why she was driving instead of flying to Reno, but not for long. It would be good to see her again.

I made short work of the breakfast and then opened the paper as I started on my coffee. The story I was looking for was on the second page. A man had been killed while driving his car the night before. One shot from a .38 through his head. His name was Tony Roma, occupation unknown, a resident of Miami, Florida.

The local police had run a make on him and he had a record. Possession of a concealed weapon, several charges of assault with a deadly weapon, and one charge of homicide, which had been dismissed for lack of evidence. No record of where he had been staying in Reno.

After I was dressed, I cleaned my gun, replaced the one shell, and put it back in the holster. I put the empty shell in my pocket and would get rid of it later. I left the hotel.

I drove downtown and stopped at the Tun bar. Don was working, and I told him to make me a drink, then went back to the public phone. I called the casino.

"Mr. Bottelli," I said when the operator answered.

There was a short pause, then a male voice answered.

"I want to talk to Angelo," I said.

"Who's calling?"

"Tell him it's March."

There was another short pause, then Bacci was on the line. "Milo," he said, "did you knock off my boy?"

"I did," I said. "Did you tell him to get me?"

"Hell, no. I told him to leave you alone. I'm not stupid enough to do a thing like that when I got more valuable things to worry about. If he tried to move in on you, he did it on his own."

"Well, he tried to move in, and I didn't want to be looking over my shoulder all the time, so I took a drive to a fairly lonely part of town. He followed and made his play. The rest you know. I just thought I'd check with you."

"It's too bad," he said. "He was a good boy, but a little too hotheaded. You leaning on Dino?"

"Not yet, but I'm going to. Heavy enough to make him know what's happened. I may even be doing you a favor. I'll see you around." I hung up and went to the bar, where my drink was waiting for me.

"How's it going?" Don asked.

"All right, I guess. At least, I'm still in the ring."

"Did you find a gold mine?"

"Found two of them. That's what they're called, anyway. Everything just looks like rocks with a yellow streak down the back. I've known some people like that, and they didn't excite me either."

"The two old boys take you up to their mine?"

"Yeah. It looked all right—if you want to swing a pickax. I don't think I'd care much for it."

"You ought to try looking for a gold mine that doesn't have to be worked."

"A pretty idea," I agreed, "but I've never encountered one. Why don't you bring me a drink and I'll listen to your story. I'll buy you one, too, so that your voice won't get all choked up with emotion."

He fixed a drink for me and brought up a bottle of beer for himself. "There has been a rumor in Reno for some time that there is between one and four tons—depending on who is repeating the rumor—of gold all neatly stacked up in bars not far from here."

"A local bank?"

"The rumor says that it's in a cave just a few miles north of Reno. That would seem to indicate that it's private property."

"Somebody saving up for a rainy day?"

"It never rains that much in Reno," he said.

"Does anybody have an idea why it's supposed to be there? Whoever owns it could sell it now for a pretty good price."

"My guess would be that it's hot," he said.

"That would be a lot of heat. Tell me, did any of your local rumormongers ever see this gold?"

He shook his head. "They'd heard there were guards all over the place."

"And nobody had ever seen the gold? They'd just heard that somebody had?"

"Well, not exactly. There was one fellow in here about three or four months ago who claimed he'd seen it. He also claimed that he had a piece of the gold and showed it to me. About the size of the head of a medium-sized nail. He said it was a core they had let him take out so he could have it examined. I saw it, but that's all I know. It might not have been gold. But it makes a good story."

"So write it up and send it to a magazine. Judging by some of the things that are printed, one of them ought to be stupid enough to buy it."

"I thought of that," he said. "There's just one thing wrong with it. Suppose the crazy story is true? What do I do if a bunch of guys come around and want to ask questions about how I know things like that? And I don't mean cops."

"Get yourself committed to a funny farm before they come around," I said. "Or produce the guy who said he'd seen it."

"He never gave his name. Said he was from Los Angeles, and he and some friends had heard about this. His friends wanted to buy it with no questions asked and smuggle it out of the country to be sold in India."

"Did he say who took him to see the gold?"

"Claimed he didn't know. Said he was taken to see it but was blindfolded. All he saw besides the gold was the insides of a cave and three tough-looking guys with guns. Then he was blindfolded again and brought back to Reno. He left town a couple of days after that, and I haven't seen him since."

"Maybe he was on a furlough from some funny farm down there." I finished my drink and stood up. "Here's the money for the two drinks plus a little for the kitty. It was a nice story, but I don't think it was worth any more than a drink. I guess I'll stick with the insurance company. I know how much money they have."

"Stick around. I'll buy you a drink."

"Thanks, Don, but some other time. I'm going down to Carson City for a couple of hours."

"What for?"

"To see if they have anybody who's saving gold bricks for a rainy day. If so, I'll introduce them to Milo, the little old rainmaker."

"Okay. Drop around anytime. I'll try to have some other stories about Reno folklore."

"Sure," I said. I went out to the car and headed for Carson City.

It was a pleasant ride and didn't take long. When I arrived, I parked and went looking for Records. I found the building right away and went in to look up the New Yukon Mining

Corporation. That didn't take long either, mostly because there wasn't much information. There were three officers, who were also the stockholders. They were Albert Nacker, Luigi Falco, and Melba Johnson. All three had the same address, which I suspected was their office.

I think I was a little disappointed that Mancetti's name hadn't been on the paper. It had been a long shot, but I'd been hoping for a little luck. But since I was there, I decided I might as well snoop around a little more. I glanced around the records room. There was nobody there except me and a stooped little old man behind a counter. He probably couldn't tell me any more than what I had read, but maybe he could fill me in on some general information. I walked over and waited for him to look up. He finally did.

"Good morning," he said. "Did you find what you wanted?"

"Part of it," I said, "but I was wondering if you could fill me in with some general information—if you're not too busy. I'm a stranger in Nevada, and I don't quite know where to learn the things I want to know."

"Where you from?"

"New York City."

"You don't say! Well, you are a piece from home. What is it you'd like to know?"

"I'm with an insurance company in New York," I said. I took out my ID and showed it to him. "We are interested in learning as much as we can about gold mines in this region. Old abandoned ones and new ones. As much of the general picture as you can and are willing to tell me. Of course, I don't want to interfere with your work—"

"Ain't very busy," he said. "Reckon I can't tell you much, but maybe as much as anyone else around here. Ain't been much gold mining around here for quite a spell. Not much of any kind of mining except copper, and that's a big operation. There ain't been much silver, although I hear that there's some new interest in it. Word is that Howard Hughes has bought up a whole bunch of old silver mines over near Virginia City, but there ain't no telling what he'll do with them.* How come you're interested?"

"We have a financial stake in a small gold mine up north of here. It's a mine which was abandoned about ninety years ago, but it's been producing fairly well for a small operation. So we are interested in the whole area."

"Got a name?"

"You mean my name? It's on the card I just showed you."

"I saw that. I mean the name of the mine north of here."

"The Natural Gold Mine. Peavine Mountain."

He frowned for a second. "I think I heard of that, but that's all. You interested in anything special around here?"

"Yes, I am—but only because I have heard that there is one that was considered worthless for a long time which only recently has begun producing again. Not big, but steadily."

"What's the name of it?"

"Well, the name of the company is the New Yukon Mining Corporation. I don't know what they're calling the mine. But I was told in Reno that they've been shipping gold out regularly."

---

* The eccentric billionaire started buying up Nevada silver mines in the late 1960s but never actually did any mining.

He nodded. "I know about it, but I can't swear that everything I've heard is gospel. It's been operating steadily for less than a year. Like you said, small. It wasn't exactly abandoned before. There was an old prospector around here who put up claim stakes on it when he got too old to go out all the time with his mule. He was also too old to work very hard, but I guess he was taking enough out of it to live on. But he was probably glad to sell out when he got the chance."

"He still around?"

"No. Left as soon as he got the money. I heard that he had some kin around San Francisco and went over there to be near them."

"That makes sense, I guess," I said. "What about the people who bought it? Local people?"

"I don't know them, but that ain't the way I hear it. I heard the two fellows are from California or somewhere like that. Now, the woman is something else. I've heard she is from here and I've heard she ain't. And that's about it."

"Is the mine near here?"

"Well, it ain't near and ain't far. Depends on whether you're walking or driving. It's just outside of Virginia City. You thinking of visiting it?"

"I thought I might try it."

"If I was you, I wouldn't just drive up and drop in on them for a visit. They might look upon it as unkindly."

"You mean they're unfriendly?"

"Folks who are sitting on top of a mine full of gold are apt to be a mite unfriendly. If I was you, I'd see if I could make an appointment to visit them. If they want you to, they'll escort you. If they don't, they'll likely be waiting with a gun to escort you away."

"Thanks for the hint," I said. "Has the new activity in the mine increased a general interest in mines?"

"Well, I heard that a couple of old mines was bought, and there's two or three new claims been staked out and recorded, but I wouldn't rightly call it a gold rush."

"Okay," I said, laughing. "Thanks for your information."

"Glad to have company. It gets a little lonely around here most days. Good luck, young fellow."

I made a friendly wave and left. The address of the New Yukon was near where I had parked my car. I climbed the stairs and entered the office. It was a pleasant, nicely furnished place—including the woman who looked at me from behind the desk. She was quite attractive with a pretty face. There was a very alive, young look about her, but I noticed the expression in her eyes was older, as though she'd been around and considered herself capable of handling anything that came up.

"Good morning," she said. There was a hint of amusement in her voice.

"It is now," I said. "A very attractive place you have here."

"I noticed you were taking inventory," she said dryly. "May I help you?"

"I'm not sure. I would like to see one of the owners."

"I'm one of the owners. Now, may I help you?"

"Let me see, now," I said gravely. "I doubt that your first name is Albert. And it couldn't be Luigi. You must be Melba Johnson."

"Clever," she said mockingly. "Now it's your turn again."

"Miss Johnson?"

"Right again. You're doing very well."

I didn't care very much for the tone of the conversation. It didn't seem to be going the way I wanted it to go. I took a deep breath and tried again.

"My name is Milo March," I said. "I'm with an insurance company in New York. We are interested in gold mines."

"How interesting, Mr. March. You are a member of a rather large group. You should never be lonely."

"Would you happen to have a Rolaid in the office, Miss Johnson?"

That startled her, but she didn't let it show too much. "Why?"

"The acid is a little thick in the office. I believe I must be allergic to it. Is your gold mine for sale?"

"No."

"Not for any price?"

"No. We like our gold mine. We like the money we make from it. It is not for sale. Even if it were, I doubt if you could afford it."

"Why don't you name a price and we'll see."

"All right, buster. Five million dollars."

"We'll take it."

"Cash?"

"Cash," I said. "All you have to do is submit an assayer's report and permit us to verify it. If you have any doubts about us, you may phone Dun and Bradstreet in New York, at my expense, and ask them about Intercontinental Insurance."

"You must be sick in the head," she snapped. She was beginning to lose her cool. "I told you that our mine isn't for sale. Don't you understand the English language?"

"I understand it—even the words you want to use but haven't gotten around to yet. Thank you for your courtesy, Miss Johnson. It has been most revealing."

I turned and walked to the door. I stopped and looked back. "One more question, Miss Johnson. If the mine isn't for sale, are you?"

Her face was no longer pretty. "Not to you, you bastard. You couldn't afford me."

"I think I could. I would have to go downstairs and buy a pack of cigarettes so I could pay your price out of the change and also give you a tip. And you might tell your partners that I think it's very smart of them not to sell a gold mine for any price—when it doesn't have any gold in it." I went out and closed the door gently. Something crashed against it as I went down the stairs.

I glanced at my watch as I got into the car. I wanted to get back to Reno before lunch, but there was one more thing I wanted to do. I headed for Virginia City.

My original plan had been to just drive to Virginia City and then to ask about the mine. But I kept my eyes open, and just before I reached the city I saw a crude sign on a side road that announced the New Yukon Mine and made it clear that it was private property. I drove about a hundred yards past it and found a place to park just off the road. I turned in and stopped the car. I glanced at my watch again. I would wait for about a half hour because I wanted to get back to Reno in time for something I wanted to do and still have time to go to the hotel and take a nap. It was going to be a long night.

I almost went to sleep while I was waiting. Then I suddenly heard the sound of a motor running in low gear. It was different enough from the motors that sped by me every few minutes to bring me fully awake. A truck came down out of the Yukon road and turned toward Virginia City. I didn't get a look at the two men in the cab, but it looked enough like the truck I had seen up on Peavine so that I started the motor and followed them.

We reached Virginia City and they turned toward Reno. This was a road that twisted around the mountains, so I didn't have to worry too much about the speed. I kept a comfortable distance behind the truck and relaxed.

When we finally reached Reno, the traffic was heavier, so I let a couple of cars get between my car and the truck, and felt pretty certain they wouldn't notice me. When we reached the end of the city limits, there was still enough traffic so there were always two or three cars between us. As we left the city limits, I noticed the reading on the speedometer.

We were ten miles out of Reno when I saw that the truck was slowing. It was signaling a left turn, so I stayed behind it. Then it turned into the narrow road of what appeared to be a small farm. I drove on past, being sure to get a good look.

There was a small, comfortable house, a barn, and a couple of smaller buildings. There were a few cattle in a fenced field, a few sheep in another, and in the background a small hill. I caught a brief glimpse of what looked like a closed opening in the hill. Then it was out of sight. I drove on for a couple of miles before I turned around. I drove straight back into Reno and put the car in a parking lot and walked to the Waldorf.

Joe brought a martini without being told. "You working?" he asked as he set it down.

"Of course, I'm working," I said indignantly. "I'm always working. It's brain work. That's why it doesn't show."

"Yeah," he said. "Sometimes, it looks as if you were short-handed." He walked away with a big grin on his face before I could think of an answer.

I sipped sullenly on the martini and started to direct my attention to the case. But that was interrupted. The door opened and Carol Chilton, the girl from Smith's office, walked in. She stopped and peered back into the restaurant, waiting for her eyes to adjust to the darkness.

"Hello," I said.

She looked around and spotted me. "Oh, hello, Milo. How are you?"

"I'm fine now. Would you care to join me in a liquid repast, or are you meeting someone?"

"No, and I will join you. Thanks." She came over and slipped onto the stool next to mine. "Aren't you working?"

"Certainly. I'm just refueling. It takes a lot of energy to keep a brain working—especially if it doesn't like to work. What about you?"

"I'm working, too. That's why I'm here. I thought I'd grab a fast drink and a sandwich to take out and go back to work. Do you suppose that they'd let me take a second martini back to the office?"

"That's easily handled," I said. Joe was already on his way up to us, so I waited.

"Hello, Carol," he said as he arrived. "You don't seem to care who you sit with, so I imagine you want a drink. The usual?"

"The young lady," I said before she could answer, "would like three things. She would like a sandwich to take back to the slave market where she works, then she would like two—not one—extra dry martinis up. Line them up. And if it's not too much of a burden, I will have one extra dry martini up. Do you think that can be managed?"

"I'll ask Jack if it's too big an order for us to handle," he said. "Watch yourself, Carol. He's a wolf."

"Please, Joe," I said quickly. "You forgot to tell her that I'm a vegetarian wolf."

"That," Joe said, "means that he only eats melons." He moved away before I could form the words. What I thought of saying was probably too obvious anyway.

"Joe likes you," she said.

"The whole establishment likes me," I said. "I don't run up tabs I can't pay. How come that slave driver you work for doesn't give you a decent lunch hour? Or two?"

"I have a lot of work to do to catch up. That's my fault, so I cut my own lunch hour."

Joe came up with the three drinks. At the same time, a waitress arrived and took the order for the sandwich to go. When she left, Carol took a deep drink of the martini. "Do you really think I can just walk out of here with the second martini?" she asked.

"The safest way," I said solemnly, "is to drink it first. The worst thing they could charge you with is drunken walking. I'm not even sure that they have a law here that covers that. I'll be your witness. Can you stand on your hands?"

"I think so. Why?"

"If they ask you to take a sobriety test by walking a straight line, tell them you can do it on your hands—and proceed to do it. I read in the local paper that some driver did that and wasn't arrested. It will probably beat the rap and it might even get you a lot of publicity. If I can borrow a camera, I'll even take the photograph and donate it to the local paper in behalf of the public weal."

"I'll bet you would," she said, "but no, thanks. How is your work coming?"

I would have been disappointed if she hadn't said that. I was expecting it. "Very well," I said confidently. "I may even get a gold star from the company."

She laughed, but her heart wasn't in it. "Seriously. Are you getting the answer to the question that was bothering you?"

"Which one?"

"I think it was something about how do you get gold out of a mine that doesn't have any gold in it."

"Oh, that one. That part of it is really very simple. You put gold in it and then you can take it out. In the old days it was much simpler. You merely got some gold dust, loaded it in a shotgun, and then fired it into the rocks in the mine. *Voilà!* There was gold. You then sold the mine and moved to another part of the country. Today it is not so simple. So the question is where do you get the gold to put in the mine so you can take it out?"

"All right. I'll bite. Where do you get the gold to put in the mine, Mister Bones?"

"I'm glad you asked. I don't know. But I have a feeling that I'm getting warm. Although that may be only because you're sitting next to me. In the meantime, I'm working."

"At what?"

"The answer to the question," I said. "That's the hardest kind of work there is."

"I don't really believe you're working," she said. She sounded annoyed. "I think it's just a pose."

"My dear," I said in hurt tones, "I will tell you in the words of a man far wiser than I: We also serve who only stand and wait. Or words like that."

She gave me a strange look. "You're a peculiar man. You do a lot of talking, but you don't say very much. And when you do, it doesn't make much sense."

I sighed heavily. "That's the story of my life. I never make any sense."

"I don't believe you," she said firmly. She reached out and touched me beneath the left arm. "Why are you carrying a gun?"

"I might have to shoot someone. It would be embarrassing if I had to shoot someone and didn't have a gun."

"You just don't want to tell me anything. Is it because I work for Mr. Smith?"

"Why should it be?" I asked in surprise. "I don't even think about him. How can you think bad things about a man named Smith? The name is as American as apple pie. Or is it as English as tipsy pudding?"

"I give up," she said. She pulled over the second martini and went to work on it. She also changed the subject, so we talked about her. I'm not sure that she was any more truthful than I had been.

Her sandwich arrived in a demure little paper bag; she paid for it and finished her martini. "Well, back to work," she said. "Thank you for the martinis, Mr. March. It was very nice talking with you."

"You took the very words out of my mouth, Miss Chilton. Don't work too hard, honey."

I watched her walk out of the restaurant. It was a pleasure. Then I became aware that Joe had walked up and was watching, too. "I agree," I said.

He laughed. "I've noticed something about you. Whenever you're working you seem to spend a lot of time girl watching. How do you get a job like that?"

"Clean living," I told him and went back to the restaurant. I had a quick lunch, then left. There were a few other things I had wanted to do, but I decided to go back to the hotel and sack out. I walked to the parking lot and drove away.

There was a message in my box at the hotel. It seemed that Mr. Belli had called and wished me to return his call. I went upstairs and asked the operator to get the number for me.

The same bored voice answered. I told her who I was and that I was returning a call from Mr. Belli. She announced that she would see if he was in. He was.

"Mr. March," he said, "Mr. Mancetti would like you to have lunch with him tomorrow."

"That's sweet of him. I'm not sure what my schedule is for

tomorrow, but if you want to tell me where and when, I'll try to be there."

"Mr. Mancetti owns a bar on South Virginia. Dino's Pub. He has to be there on business and he suggested that you meet him there about eleven-thirty, and then he'll take you to lunch."

"I can hardly wait," I said. "Tell him I'll be there if I can make it." I hung up. Within ten minutes I was asleep.

NINE

When I awakened, I was hungry. My first thought was that I'd better call down and order breakfast. It was the day that Mei was to arrive. I swung my legs out of bed and reached for a cigarette. After it was lit, I looked around the room. There was something wrong. Sunlight was coming faintly through the window. That was it. The window faced west. It wasn't morning. I glanced at my watch. It was six o'clock. Then I remembered. I had returned to the hotel early and gone to sleep because it was the night I was going back to the mountain with Ambrose and Necktie.

I got out of bed and went over to the table. I mixed myself a drink of gin and grapefruit juice and sat down. There wasn't any ice but I didn't miss it. I finished the drink, got dressed in my mountain clothes, and went downstairs. I had a leisurely dinner and then went out to the jeep.

I stopped at a delicatessen downtown where I bought several sandwiches and a big bottle of bourbon, and dry ice to pack around it. Then I went straight to Ambrose's house.

They were both sitting in the living room waiting for me. There were three drinks on the table. Necktie jumped up. "Thought you'd be here about this time," he said, "but I might have guessed it a mite later. I'll get you some ice."

"It looks like it's still cold enough," I said. I sat down and lit a cigarette. "You boys eat yet?"

"Yeah," Ambrose said, "but Necktie can rustle up some more for you if you're hungry."

"I had dinner at the hotel," I said. I picked up my drink and sipped it. "But we have plenty of time. You said that they usually leave their mine late. I think they'll be even later tonight."

"Why?"

"I had a phone call today," I said. "Dino Mancetti wants to have lunch with me tomorrow. It's easy to guess why. He knows that I'm onto something and that I'm getting closer to him all the time. That means that he has to rush out the last of his bricks. And there's another reason."

"What's that?"

"There's another man here in Reno. He is just as much interested in what Dino is doing as I am. And if he also stumbles onto anything, he won't go to the cops. He'll act more directly."

"You mean kill him or something?" Necktie asked.

"Something," I agreed.

"Why?"

"I'm not quite sure," I admitted, "but I think I'll get the answer tonight." I finished my drink. "Ready to go?"

"Guess so," Ambrose said. He and Necktie put on their heavy jackets, and we went out to the jeep.

"I don't imagine we have to be in a big hurry tonight," I said. "We'll go the long way. And it's more comfortable. I'm not sure that I remember the way. You'll let me know where to turn, Ambrose?"

"Sure."

It was a fairly long drive, but the traffic was light and I was making good time. Finally we were up on the mountain and heading for what had once been Poeville. The only lights showing anywhere were from the jeep. Then ahead of us I saw a slight widening in the road. I eased up on the accelerator. "That's it ahead, isn't it?" I asked. "We turn left?"

"Correct," Ambrose said. "Then we go about halfway up to the mines. I'll tell you where to stop."

I swung to the left, shifted gears, and started up the hill. I drove slowly, partly to keep the engine noise down. Then I spotted bushes on the left side of the road.

"That's the place," Ambrose said. "Turn there and drive in behind the bushes. That way, if they're still up there, they won't see the car when they drive down. That's the way you want it, ain't it?"

"That's the way." I turned the wheel and ran the car in behind the bushes. There was plenty of room, and the ground there was fairly flat. I braked the car to a stop. "Is that far enough?" I asked Ambrose.

"Plenty," he said.

I turned off the lights, stopped the motor, and we got out. I picked up the bag containing the bourbon and the sandwiches and also got a flashlight which I had put in the jeep the day before.

"We better chunk the wheels with a couple of rocks," Necktie said. "That way we don't have to worry about the jeep suddenly deciding to roll back down the hill."

"I set the brakes," I said. "What could cause that?"

"A couple of things," Ambrose said. "We don't get many of them, but there could be a little quake that would just be enough to give it a shove. Or a varmint might run into it."

I switched on the flashlight and held it until Ambrose and Necktie found a couple of rocks and wedged them behind the rear wheels.

"Shut it off now," Ambrose said. "Necktie and me know the rest of the road like the back of our hands. We usually leave our truck down at the bottom and walk the rest of the way. But we don't want no lights, no talking, or no kind of noise the rest of the way. Me and Necktie will go ahead and you follow us. Just as we get to the bend up ahead, we'll stop and I'll take a look around the curve and see if it's clear. If it is, I'll motion and we'll go ahead. They might be loading their truck, and if they are, then we got to get into my mine between trips. Don't make no noise."

They moved out and I followed. I could barely make out their outlines, although they weren't very far ahead of me. There were loose pebbles underfoot, and I followed along, stumbling and biting my lips to keep from swearing.

Finally we were at the top and Ambrose was vaguely silhouetted against the sky as he raised his hand for me to stop. A moment later, he gestured for me to come on.

There was a very dim light in front of the door to the other mine. The truck was parked in front, but there was no one in sight. The door was partly open, we could see lights coming from the mine, and there was the sound of voices.

We hurried across to Ambrose's mine, and he unlocked the door. We stepped inside and Ambrose draped the chain and lock so that to the casual glance it would seem to be locked. I turned on the flashlight, holding it close to the ground, and we went into the far chamber. Ambrose picked up one of the carbide lanterns and lit it, placing it at the far end.

"It won't show out through the door from there," he said, keeping his voice low. "I reckon we shouldn't do too much talking and better keep it low when we do."

"Why?" Necktie wanted to know.

"Well, I ain't giving no credit to your fancy idea that there's a hole between their mine and this one, but if you're right, then they could hear everything we said in here, maybe even if we was talking low."

"What if they did?" Necktie said. "We got a right to be here."

"Yeah. But there ain't much we can do about our right if there's a bullet hole in us."

"Wait a minute," I said. "Listen."

There was the sound of a motor starting up outside. There were also voices, but we couldn't hear what they were saying. A minute later there was the clash of gears, and then the truck moved slowly away. It was driving in low gear, and the sound of the motor faded slowly as it crept down the mountain.

"Hot dog," Necktie said. "This is my chance "

"Wait, you damn fool," Ambrose said. "They probably left a man behind with a gun, and he can pick you off the minute you stick your head inside that mine."

"Ain't no bullet going to kill me. You're forgettin' that my old pappy said I was born to be hanged."

He disappeared into the next chamber. Ambrose and I were

just about to follow when we heard the scream. It quickly choked off in a sob and then there was no sound—except that of a far-off bird.

TEN

Necktie had been right about one thing. There was certainly a hole between the two mines and it was masked by the bushes. His father had been right about one thing, too. Necktie may not have been born for that specific reason, but it was hanging that had killed him even if he wasn't dangling in the air. I thought that Necktie must have died happy, knowing that his father had not missed on a single prophecy.

Ambrose, though shaken, left to call the sheriff's office while I went back into the other chamber and poured a drink. I sat on the stool and sipped it, thinking about the situation. I had no idea how long it would take the cops to get there. It was the middle of the night and we were a hell of a way up in the mountain. But I supposed that murder would bring them as quickly as they could make it. And there were things I wanted to do before they arrived and even before Ambrose got back. I finished the drink, took the flashlight, and walked out of the mine.

It was cold, even though I was warmly dressed. I walked over to the door of the mine next door. There was a heavy chain with a big padlock on it. It might have been difficult to break, but it was easy to pick. I had it open in a matter of seconds. I went inside and turned on the flashlight. There wasn't much to see. There was some equipment which looked similar to what Ambrose had in his mine. There was something else which I didn't recognize but I guessed it was for the purpose of melting down gold. Near it was a huge storage battery to which it was connected. I also noticed that there were two light fixtures in the ceiling that were also connected to it.

I didn't bother trying to find a switch for the lights. I used my flashlight to tour slowly around the walls. I probably wouldn't have known any gold if I'd seen it, but I didn't see any signs that there had been any digging recently.

Finally I was back at the machine I suspected was for melting gold. I glanced inside of it. There was no sign there or elsewhere of finely broken or ground-up rock. Everything was spick-and-span. I stood there and flashed my light around. There was the matching bunch of bushes to what was in the other mine, and I could see the rope stretching up to a two-by-four overhead. I didn't have to look to see what was attached to the other end. It was Necktie.

I flashed the light around again and noticed what looked like a bundle of sacks near the machine. I kicked them idly and it hurt.

I bent down to pick them up. It was one sack, but there was something heavy in it. I took a look. Inside there were three gold bricks. I was about to leave them, but then I suddenly noticed something that was different. There wasn't a pair of dice stamped on them. Instead there were initials and a number. I had a hunch about that. I picked up the mouth of the sack and dragged it over to the door and outside.

Closing the padlock again, I dragged the sack over beyond

Ambrose's mine. There was a pile of rocks there. I put the sack and its contents next to the rocks and pushed several rocks on top of it. Satisfied with the way it looked, I went back into Ambrose's mine. I moved the carbide lantern into the back chamber and set it down.

I had noticed something when I was there before which had made me curious. It had nothing to do with the case I was on, but I was going to try to look into it. There was a section of the rock wall some distance from where Ambrose and Necktie had been digging where a large section of rock was very black. They had explained it to me as being the result of water seeping down through the earth and rock. They probably knew what they were talking about, but I had been thinking about it. If the water was the only cause, then the whole wall should have been the same color. I had a little time and I was going to find out why.

There was a pickax on the floor and I picked it up. I don't know how long it took, but I finally had a fair section of rock outlined by the pick. I put it down and took up a sharp-edged crowbar and a short-handled sledgehammer. I went to work on that section. I was already getting tired when I felt the crowbar go in deeper than it had before. I put down the hammer and went to work on prying with the crowbar.

Finally, something gave and a large hunk of rock tumbled loose and fell to the floor, almost hitting me on the foot. I muttered a few choice words, threw down the crowbar, and bent over to look at the piece of rock I had pried out. I couldn't see anything. I went back to get the flashlight and returned to the rock. There wasn't anything to see at first, but then I turned the rock over. There was a big, broad streak of yellow running through the entire length of the rock.

I stood up and used the flashlight to look into the hole from which the rock had come. The same streak of yellow stretched out from both ends. There was more yellow in the back, but not as heavy. I thought I was immune to such things, but I felt excitement at seeing it. I didn't know anything about the business, but I felt as if a Madison Avenue character had just discovered gold.

When I finally got over the first excitement of the idea of finding gold, I picked up the rock and took it outside. I put it in the sack with the gold bars and arranged the sack the same way it had been. Then I went back and poured myself a big drink of bourbon. I felt I had earned it.

I drank the first one fast and poured another. I sipped it slowly while I thought over what I had discovered. I was pleased by the idea that Ambrose's mine might be worth more than he thought, and that now it was all strictly for him. I knew that Necktie had been his only friend and was even more important to him than gold. He would need some incentive to go on after what I'd found. But news of it would have to wait until I could check the sample the following day.

I was also pleased by what I had discovered in the other mine. There were a few other things to be done, but I knew that the case was really solved. Though I would have to tie up loose ends, I was glad that I had broken the back of the case before Mei arrived.

The door to the mine creaked open. "Milo?" he called. It was Ambrose.

"I'm back here," I called. I poured a drink for him as the door was closing with a protest.

He looked old and tired as he came in. He sat down on the stool and took a long drink, with the air of a man who needed it rather than one who enjoyed it.

"Necktie?" he asked.

"He's still there and still dead," I said. "I'm sorry, Ambrose. In a way it's my fault. If I hadn't asked the two of you to bring me up here, it wouldn't have happened."

He shook his head. "No. I was thinking about it while I was gone. I reckon it wouldn't have made any difference. I don't guess that Necktie ever thought about anything but his pappy's prediction since the time he was a little tyke. If it hadn't happened now, it would have still happened. He was thinking about it every day. But I'll miss him."

"I know," I said softly. "I'll miss him myself. And they were mean people. The rope that's around Necktie's neck is tied to a two-by-four in the next mine. Necktie was right. There is a hole between the two mines. They could have easily blocked up the hole. Instead they set a spring trap like you would for an animal. But they'll pay for it. That's the reason I insisted that we not disturb the body. Did you reach the sheriff?"

He nodded. "They'll be here as soon as they can. Reckon they ought to be here soon. A half hour, maybe an hour."

"We'll wait. Then we'll leave as soon as they let us. You must be tired."

"A mite," he admitted. "Did you find anything important next door?"

"Yes. I found the answer to the most important question of

all. One I have been asking myself over and over. And it is so simple I should have thought of it before."

"What was that?"

"How do you get gold out of a mine that doesn't have any gold in it?"

"Well, I guess you could salt the mine. But that's only good if you're trying to make a quick sale of it."

"Right," I said. "So it had to be something different. It was the most obvious answer in the world, but I didn't stumble on to it until tonight. You bring gold into the mine, then take it out again."

"I don't get it." He looked even more tired, and I hoped that the police would come soon.

"Suppose," I said, "you had some stolen gold which you could not easily sell. You then buy a mine and move in. You bring in your stolen gold, melt it down, and remold it into bricks with your own mark on it, and then sell it as if you'd mined it and processed it. You can sell it openly without any trouble. And that's all there is to it."

His face showed he was finally listening. "Yeah. That's right. But who around here has any stolen gold and how would they handle it? And where would the stolen gold come from?"

"I don't have the answer to the last question," I said. I stood up and pretended to search my pockets. "I'm out of cigarettes. I'll get some from the jeep and be right back." I turned around and left.

Ambrose had parked the jeep right in front of the mine as I had expected. I picked up the sack with the gold bars and the sample of ore from Ambrose's mine and put them under the seat in the jeep. Then I went back into the mine, lighting a cigarette as I went.

Ambrose had already poured himself another drink and was listlessly working at it. I sat down and poured myself another drink and took a sip.

"Want a sandwich?" I asked.

"Nope. Don't exactly feel like it."

"Okay. We'll wait for the police to come. It shouldn't take long and then we'll go home. Don't say anything to them about me being inside the other mine. It has nothing to do with their work."

"Whatever you say, Milo," he said. It was obvious that he wasn't even thinking about it.

We had two more drinks without talking, and then finally the men from the sheriff's office arrived. There was an ambulance with them. We went out to meet them.

It didn't take long. They looked at Necktie. One of them took photographs of Necktie. They broke the lock on the other mine and took photographs from in there. They carried Necktie out and put him in the ambulance. Then one of them asked Ambrose and me a few questions. He was a little curious about me when he found out I was from New York, but I explained that I worked for an insurance company that had some mining interests in the West and that Ambrose had been teaching me a little about gold mining, and that seemed to satisfy him. He also asked a few questions about who owned the other mine, and we told him the little we knew. Then they took off.

"Let's go, Ambrose," I said. "You look tired, and it'll be damned near morning when we get back to Reno."

"I guess," he said.

We both had a quick drink and then carried the bottle and the sandwiches out to the jeep. We climbed in and I started the motor, turned around, and started down the hill.

"I'm going to miss that danged fool," he said sadly. That was the last thing he said until we got back to his house. I stopped in front of the house and lifted up the bag that had the bourbon and sandwiches in it.

"Here, take this," I said. "You'll probably need a drink or two. And if you get hungry later, you can have a sandwich so you don't have to bother with cooking anything. I'm sorry about Necktie."

"Yep," he said. "I'm going to miss the little fool. He kind of growed on me."

"He did on me, too," I admitted. "You going to be home today, Ambrose?"

"Yep. Got no place to go, I reckon."

"I'll be up to see you sometime later," I said. "Try to get some sleep. You must be knocked out."

"I'm a mite tuckered," he said. He picked up the bag and climbed out of the jeep. "Good night, Milo."

"Good night, Ambrose," I said gently. I felt as if there was something else I should say, but I knew it wouldn't do any good. I watched him walk heavily into the house, then turned the jeep around and headed downtown.

Streaks of daylight were beginning to show over the mountain as I reached the hotel. I took the sack from under the seat, bundled it up as well as I could, and put it under my arm, trying to act as if it wasn't heavy as I walked inside. I went straight to the elevator and went upstairs. First I put the sack in one of the closets and covered it with some clothes that needed to go to the laundry.

After I had taken off my jacket, I made myself a drink and sat down. I was tired but I decided I'd better eat something. I phoned room service and ordered breakfast. I left the door partly open and went over and sat down at the table where I could see the sunrise.

The knock came on the door and I called out for him to come in. He entered and brought the tray over to the table. He put my breakfast down and then produced a newspaper. "I'm sorry, sir," he said, "but the morning paper has not yet been delivered. I thought you might like to see last night's paper."

"Thanks," I said dryly. I took the check, added a tip, and signed it. As he walked out with it, I saw he was smiling. He was probably thinking about all the improvements on his new house.

After finishing breakfast, I undressed and went over to sit on the bed. I lit a cigarette and finally picked up the tele-phone receiver. I asked the operator to get the San Francisco office of the FBI. She gasped and wanted to know if there was anything wrong.

"No," I said cheerfully, "everything is just fine. Now, if I may have the number called ..." She took the hint, but I would have been willing to bet that she'd be listening in.

I heard the phone ringing and then it was picked up and a man answered.

"The FBI?" I asked.

"What do you want?"

"My name is Milo March. I am staying at the Pony Express Hotel in Reno. You have a man named Frank Newton. I want to talk to him. Tell him he can call me here anytime during the next three hours. After that, he can call and leave a number where I can reach him. Tell him that I said it's important."

"What is it about?"

"I'll tell Frank," I said and hung up.

I waited a minute and then got the operator back and asked her to be sure and call me in three hours. I put the cigarette out and went to sleep.

The phone awakened me. I fought my way up out of a deep sleep and reached for the phone with one hand while I reached for a cigarette with the other.

"Hello," I said, trying to sound alert.

"Milo?"

"Yeah."

"This is Frank," he said. "How are you?"

"Sleepy. I can't seem to get enough sleep. Where are you? San Francisco?"

"Yes."

"Can you take a run over to Reno? I've got something that's right in your backyard."

"What?"

"I'd rather not say on the telephone. But it's hot and it's big and it's your baby if you want it. It is also Federal."

"I can catch a plane and be at your hotel in less than two hours. Will that be all right?"

"Fine," I said, "but don't stretch it much beyond that. I have a luncheon date with one of the main characters. I'll wait here for you."

"Okay," he said and hung up.

I felt a little better. He was a nice guy—for a cop. An idea about the whole case had been forming in my head since the middle of the night before, and it would be pretty well set by the time he arrived. I went into the bathroom, shaved and showered, and then went back to the table by the window. I mixed myself a drink and decided to look over the paper the waiter had left with my breakfast.

There wasn't much in it that was very exciting. But finally in the center of the paper there was a short story I found more interesting. Three men had been killed a few miles north of Reno. They had not yet been identified. The bodies had been found in an open field. Each man had been shot through the back of the head.

Somehow it sounded to me like a gang killing, which was why I found it interesting. It just might fit in with the picture I had been building in my mind.

I decided to go downstairs and have a second breakfast. On the way I stopped at the desk. There was a telegram for me. I carried it into the restaurant, where I ordered a martini and scrambled eggs with ham. Then I opened the telegram. It was from Mei. She said that she would be in Reno between five and six o'clock.

While I waited for my order to be delivered, I leaned back and thought about Mei. It would be nice to see her again and to know that I could see her for a few days and nights. I would also have time enough to do some work before she arrived. Enough so that I might be able to finish the case the next day. Or at least the day after.

I finished my second breakfast and left the restaurant. On the way to the elevator I stopped and bought the morning paper. I picked up a bucket of ice cubes and went up to my room. I fixed myself a drink and sat down with the paper. The story was also in the morning news, but it wasn't any different. Still no identification.

So I read the comics and waited. Finally the phone rang and I crossed the room to answer it. It was the desk clerk. "There is a Mr. Frank Newton here to see you, Mr. March."

"Tell him to come up," I said. I put down the receiver and took the gold bricks from the sack on the floor. I carried them across to the table and set them down. Then I laid the newspaper carefully over them and picked up my drink.

A knock came on the door a few minutes later. I walked over and opened it.

"Hello, Milo," he said.

"Hello, Frank. It's good to see you."

"I hope so," he said. "Somebody in the office wanted to know if you were the new regional director of the agency."

"You could do worse," I said modestly. "Want a drink?"

"I'm on duty—I think."

"Not quite yet. All you have to do is listen to me for the moment. If you can, I want you to stay for at least a day and then I think you can wrap up the whole thing. But, if I'm right, you'll need some help."

"Besides you?" he asked dryly.

"Not on the brain work, just on the physical action. What about a drink? It's almost lunchtime."

He laughed. "Okay. I'll have a martini."

I called room service and ordered two of them. I went back to the table and finished my drink. "If you want to see the latest news, always pick up the newspaper and look."

He picked up the paper and stared down at the bricks for a couple of seconds. "Pretty," he said. "You mentioned it was hot. Does that mean you lifted these?"

"No. I borrowed them from the people who did. I figured you'd need some evidence."

"Considerate of you. What's the story?"

"Wait until we get our drinks. You might drape the newspaper tastefully over the evidence again. The room service waiter has big eyes, and I have a theory he's planning on building a new house and will take financing from anywhere he can get it."

He put the paper back and we waited. Finally there was the polite tap on the door. I walked over and opened it. It was my regular waiter.

"Just put them on the dresser," I said. "And give me the check."

"Yes, sir. I took the liberty of bringing you the morning paper since there wasn't one when I brought you your breakfast."

"I bought one," I told him. I waited while he put down the tray and handed me the check. I added the tip and gave it back to him.

"Thank you, sir. Is there anything else?"

"Yes. Close the door gently as you leave. I have a headache."

He looked hurt, but as he turned he glanced at the check and the look was replaced by a smile. When he was gone, I carried the two drinks over to the table and threw the paper to one side.

"You know anything about hot gold?"

"I know there is such a thing. I haven't worked on any, but there has been some in the office."

"Do the stampings on those bricks mean anything? They should tell where the gold came from."

"They probably do, but I'll have to check with the office. Where did you get these?"

"They were lying under an old sack in a mine up in the mountain. I was in there last night and found them. The mine has been inactive for many years. Recently three men took it over and formed a corporation. They've supposedly been working the mine since then and they have been selling gold bricks regularly to a broker here in Reno. Bricks with their mark stamped on them."

"What does that have to do with these bricks?"

"I entered the mine last night when there was no one there. I will bet that it is many years—maybe a hundred—since anyone did any mining there. They had considerable equipment in the mine, but the only thing that had been used was a machine to melt down gold and molds for making bricks. Nothing else.

"So," I continued, "let us suppose that someone has a goodly amount of gold bricks which have been stolen and cannot be sold in any legitimate market in this country. So he gets hold of an old abandoned mine, gets an assayer to give a good report on it, and starts producing gold. He moves gold bricks in, melts them down, and molds new bricks on which he puts his own mark. Then he sells them to a legal buyer as the fruits of his labor in his mine. Everything seems perfectly legal. Nice, huh?"

"Yeah," Frank said. "It would work unless someone happened along and stumbled onto it. How come you're in the picture?"

"I stumbled along," I said dryly. "The men who own the mine used an assayer's report and a sample of something supposed to be gold ore to take out an insurance policy for two million dollars to protect themselves against the possibility of the mine not being as good as the assayer said it was. They have demanded payment on the policy."

"Your company?"

"My company. They're like a lot of people. They get gold spots in front of their eyes. So they didn't investigate properly before they issued the policy. They were thinking about those beautiful big premiums. So when the roof fell in, they screamed for me."

"You know where this stolen gold is hidden?"

"I think I knew where it was yesterday. But it may not be there today. At least not all of it. The rumors are that there are a thousand tons of gold hidden somewhere near Reno."

"Know who's back of it?"

"I know who's fronting this mine, and I have a good idea who's really back of it. You ever hear of Dino Mancetti?"

Frank frowned for a minute. "Yeah, I've heard of him. He's in our files, but there isn't much on him. He's not very big. He runs one of the three legal houses of prostitution in this part of Nevada. That's about it. He does belong to one of the big Syndicate families back East, which is the only reason we have a file on him. Why?"

"He and two other men own the corporation that has the mine here. They are the ones who have the insurance policy. And I think that Mancetti may have been the custodian for the stolen gold and that the gold is actually the possession of the Syndicate."

"You're beginning to interest me more," Frank said. "Do you remember Angelo Bacci from Las Vegas? You helped me to put him away once."

"I remember him. I met him a second time in Florida. I didn't manage to put him in a hospital. Now he's in Reno."

Frank whistled softly. "It must be a secret. There hasn't been any mention of it in the newspapers or in any reports I've seen."

"He's here under the name of Joseph Bottelli. Two of his pet hoods were with him. He had someone call me and invite me to come to his suite for cocktails. He was more or less friendly but told me that he'd heard I was bothering Mancetti and he'd take it as a personal favor if I'd lay off. He claimed that Mancetti was legitimately mining gold and that he felt like a brother toward Mancetti. That made me certain that I was on the trail of something more than mere insurance fraud."

"It was all that friendly?"

"I don't know," I said. "It may have been an order or it may have been purely personal, but one of his hoods came after me. He had the hotel staked out when I came back at night. So I changed cars and took a little drive. He followed me. I deliberately drove to a part of town where he would have a chance, if that was what he wanted. He took the chance to kill me."

"What happened?"

"I killed him," I said.

Frank shook his head. "Didn't you ever learn the basic things about your business? You're not supposed to go around laying traps so you can kill someone."

"I started out by learning this business in the engine room. I learned two things. To solve the case I'm on and to stay alive. Besides, it was his trap and he had a gun in his hand when I shot him."

"Do the police know about this?"

"They know that he was killed if they read the newspapers. If they ever ask me anything about it, I'll tell them, but I never was much for running around carrying tales."

He sighed and shook his head again. "All right. I'll forget what I heard. Incidentally, you'll be interested to know that Mancetti is part of Bacci's family."

"I must be getting old. I should have guessed that when he pulled that 'brother' line on me. If I'm right about who the gold belongs to, then that's the reason he's out here. He may even suspect the same thing I do."

"What's that?"

"If Mancetti is playing custodian and is also acting as middleman on selling the gold, he probably is getting a percentage on what he sells. A small one. But I suspect something else. I think that Mancetti is also siphoning off some of the gold so that he can keep all of the money from the extra slice."

"How?"

"I discovered by accident that someone else is selling gold from Reno. Also derived from an old gold mine which is suddenly producing again. It is near Virginia City. It is also owned by three people. They're putting their gold into bricks and trucking them to Reno and shipping them to a broker in San Francisco. The mine is owned by the New Yukon Mining Corporation, and the officers and stockholders are Albert Nacker, Luigi Falco, and Melba Johnson. The two men are believed to be from California. Nobody seems quite sure where Miss Johnson is from. My guess would be from the nearest whorehouse."

"Is there a point to this?" Frank asked.

"There may be. After my investigation in Carson City, I drove over near Virginia City and parked near a private road which was marked as the property of the New Yukon. I had some time to kill and thought I might get a lucky break, and I did. A truck came down that road and headed for Reno. It was the same truck that made all the trips to and from the mine up on Peavine."

"You think there's a connection with Mancetti?"

"I do. Otherwise why would the truck be there? I think it may have delivered a load of gold bars, with the same stamp as those in front of you, so that they could be melted and then molded into other bars with a Yukon stamp on them. I think that the three owners are fronts for Dino and that the gold that comes from that mine is part of the stash near Reno and is a part of the gold that is being shipped from there without the knowledge or consent of Bacci and his peers."

"How much has been sold out of the two mines?"

"About one million dollars from each mine."

"All right," Frank said. "You've sold me. What are your plans?"

I glanced at my watch. "I have to leave here within a few minutes and go to keep my luncheon date with Dino Mancetti. I intend to shake him up a little. I'm certain that he has already started to move the original gold which is still left. But it will take several trips. The truck they have is not large enough to be able to move it fast. Also, it's safer if they do most of the moving at night."

"I'll catch a plane back to San Francisco right away. I can clear it with the Bureau and also find out where this gold came from. We have agents we can use from here and Carson City, and I can arrange for more from San Francisco. I can be back here early this evening. Why not raid them then?"

"No," I said strongly. "I would like it if you'd do it tomorrow. You'll get a bigger haul, and it will also help me."

"Those are your only reasons?"

"No," I admitted. "I'll tell you the other reasons in a minute. First, I am going to have lunch with Mancetti and shake him up a little more. Then, sometime this afternoon, I am going in to make charges against Mancetti and the two men with him. Conspiracy to commit grand larceny to the extent of two million dollars against Intercontinental Insurance. I want to try to get them held in jail until tomorrow. That should keep them until I can settle my end of it."

"Maybe I can help with that. If it's worth it."

"It is. The three of them may also be charged with murder before the end of the day. It should make them push the panic button. They have to make sure that the gold is moved out tonight. They'll be more afraid of Bacci than they are of the cops. And tomorrow morning I will give them a small ray of hope by dropping my charge against them in return for a quitclaim."

"That's your end of it. What about ours?"

"I'm coming to it, Frank. I have a couple of other things to do this afternoon. Then I have to be back here between five and six. A girlfriend of mine is arriving from Hong Kong. About dusk, I'm going to take her for a drive out in the country. I expect to see a truck leaving from the place I know about and driving to a new place. I intend to follow and see where it's going."

"Why not let us raid it before they move it?"

"Because I want it this way. I promised you there would be a bonus. But it's done my way or not at all."

"Milo," he said heavily, "I could arrest you. For withholding evidence and conspiracy in a felony. You know that."

I smiled at him. "Sure, I know it. But you couldn't make it stick. And they'd laugh at you if you merely told them what I've outlined to you. And you'd not only lose what I've put in front of you, but you would also lose Bacci."

"What's that mean?"

"It means that I think I can have Bacci on the spot when you do raid. If you do it as I say."

"Do you realize that I could be thrown out of the Bureau

on my ass for even listening to you about what you think I should do?"

"I know it. But I also know that I'm right. I also know that I have to do all the front work and you have to provide the rear action. But don't forget you'll get all the credit if it works."

"Big deal," he said. "How do I know you can deliver?"

"Who delivered Bacci to you in Las Vegas? And took a bullet doing it?"

"You did," he admitted. "What I don't get is why you're so worked up about all this. You admit that you have your own case all sewed up. What are you so hot about?"

"I'll tell you," I said. "There was an old man killed last night. A nice old man who never harmed anybody and never had anything very good handed to him. There were two old men. One of them owned a gold mine right next to Mancetti's mine. That old man took in the homeless old man. The two of them worked the mine together and managed to take out enough gold to keep them in groceries, clothes, and whiskey and to pay the taxes and utilities on the ramshackle house where they lived. They did that by dint of work too hard for them. They were friends and they tried to take care of each other. One of them was killed last night."

"Which one?"

"The second one. His name was Johnny Murphy. When he was a little boy his father, who loved to make predictions, made one about him. He said that his son was 'born to be hanged.' So when the boy grew up, everyone started calling him Necktie. In a way, he was proud of this. But he was a born loser and never made anything of himself. He probably didn't eat regularly until the other man took him in. And he died last night—with a rope around his neck. Hanged to death, even though his feet weren't off the ground."

"How?"

"There was an opening between the two mines, covered on both sides by underground shrubbery. Somebody had put a snare in that opening. Necktie tripped the snare and was dead before we could get to him. Bacci probably never heard of him. Maybe Mancetti never did either. But the two men who were running the mine knew him. Necktie had never done anything to them. But they killed him, just as surely as if they had done it face to face. And the first old man is heartbroken because he lost his only friend. And I'm going to see that they pay for it, and I don't care whether it's in a prison or in front of a gun. My gun. Does that answer your question?"

I stopped talking and pulled a cigarette out of the pack in my pocket. I lit it and took a pull on it. "I'm sorry, Frank. I didn't mean to give a sermon—but I meant every word of it. And that's why it has to be done my way. And to do it, I'll fight you and the whole FBI. Now it's up to you."

I reached over and snared the bottle of gin and the orange juice. There were still a few small ice cubes floating around in the bucket. I pulled some out and mixed a drink for myself. I looked at Frank and he nodded. I mixed a drink for him and shoved it across to him. He took the glass and lifted it. We both drank.

"I know all about you," he said. "You think you're a hard guy, but you've got a heart like warm putty. I just wanted to know what you really had in mind and how far you were willing to go. I could be fired for this, too, but I'll go along with you."

"Thanks, Frank," I said.

"Anything else you want to tell me?"

"Yeah. There's a guy in town whose name is Manfred Smith. He has an office on South Virginia Street. He's a lawyer and an assayer. He has to be involved in some way with this gold scam. My company sent out an investigator to look things over when they were first approached about the policy. He naturally looked for an expert opinion. I don't know how he found this Smith, but I suspect he was steered to him. Anyway, Smith's report claimed that there were several million dollars in gold in the mine. Like I said, Intercontinental couldn't see anything but the dollar signs on the premiums and accepted his report."

"I'll check him out. Where are you meeting Mancetti for lunch?"

"He owns a bar down on South Virginia. Dino's Pub. I'm to meet him there and then we'll go someplace for lunch."

"You want a cover?"

"No."

"Okay. You said you're going to make a charge of fraud against him and his associates. When are you intending to do that?"

"I don't know. The only thing I'm certain about is that I want the three of them thrown into jail sometime today and kept there until tomorrow. By that time, there should be a murder charge against them, too. But I want them to spend the night in jail."

He sighed. "Well, I'm already sticking my neck out, so I might as well stick it out a little farther. What time do you want them picked up today?"

"I'd like to see him first. Then he can be picked up anytime—as long as the three of them stay in jail until I see them tomorrow. I don't want them getting out on bail as soon as they're picked up."

"The names of the other two men?"

"Jerry Lake and Nick Lancer. I haven't seen Lake, but I have seen Lancer. My bet is that he's a gun."

"And the name of the corporation?"

"The Natural Gold Mine Corporation of Nevada."

"Offices in Reno?"

"Yes. And the gold was sold to a broker here in town. His name is Poe."

"Okay. You have to go to your luncheon date, and I have to do a couple of things here and then fly back to San Francisco, set up everything with the office, get some clothes, and come back. I'll take a room here before I leave. What time did you say you'd be back here?"

"I should be here by five o'clock. My friend is supposed to be here between five and six. She's one of those women who have the unpleasant habit of being on time."

"I should be back by then. If I'm in the hotel, I'll leave a message for you. Before I leave, I'll take care of your three friends. I'll have them picked up on suspicion, and they won't have to be charged until tomorrow. That will keep them in jail for about twenty-four hours. That should be enough time for you."

"Plenty. Thanks, Frank."

"If you deliver what you promise, that will be plenty for me. By the way, how do you expect to deliver Bacci?"

"Easy, I think. A thousand tons of gold isn't something that's apt to be lifted by any small house burglar. It makes sense that it is in the hands of the Syndicate. You agree?"

"It's logical."

"Bacci's presence also fits in. I'm sure he didn't come here for a vacation. In fact, he told me he was here on business. I can't imagine any other kind of business that would lure him here and cause him to be registered under another name. And there is another factor which I find interesting."

"What?"

"Yesterday's paper had a short item on three unidentified men who had been killed just north of Reno. The description of the killing sounded like a hood job. That is also reasonable. I doubt if Bacci would trust even a member of his family to be custodian of that much gold without making certain that it was protected from his good friend as well as from the outside. My guess would be that he would import some of his men to guard the gold twenty-four hours a day. My guess would be that he'd have three men on guard for every eight hours. The three men who were killed were part of that."

"That makes sense," he said. "And that leaves six. They may have been bought off, but there were three who remained loyal."

"That's it. Now, as soon as I find out where the gold is being moved, I will pay a little visit to Angelo. I will tell him an imaginary story about some gold. He'll connect it up. This will be after I find out where the gold is being moved and I have told you. And I will tell Bacci where it is. You can be sure he'll go after it. You then have the place staked out and you hit a jackpot."

"Sounds good," Frank said. "Only one thing. Why should Bacci believe you instead of suspecting a trap?"

"He thinks I'm more friendly than I am. He swears that he didn't order his man to try to kill me, and I think I believe him. The man had been a close friend of a man who died in Florida as the result of wounds which I gave him. Bacci will think that I'm repaying him for not having sent the man after me and for not wanting to get even because I killed the other man. He thinks like that. He also hopes that he can still hire me."

"Why don't you take the job?" Frank asked curiously.

"I don't like the company I'd have to keep. Also, I'm sure he wouldn't pay enough money."

"You mean that you make more money than the Syndicate would pay you?"

"Yes. I normally get three hundred dollars per diem plus expenses. On some cases, I get a percentage of what I save the company. I believe that in this case it will mean twenty thousand dollars. And I'm not hired to kill. I kill someone when it is necessary to save my own life. Even then, if I have time, I try to wound them. Sometimes I kill people who merely need it. Take Bacci. Once I shot him and tried to only wound him and hurt him. The second time I tried to kill him.* If there's a

---

* The first time Milo shot Bacci (in the knee) was in *Green Grow the Graves*. The second time was in *The Bonded Dead*.

third time, I will try the same thing. You should understand that. I never heard of an FBI man who deliberately missed a man who was trying to kill him."

"Okay," he said. "We'll drop the subject. We have a rough outline of what we're going to do. Do you have something that I can put around these gold bars? I'd hate to carry them through the hotel like this."

"They'd probably think you were merely a high roller. I do have something, if it'll make you more comfortable." I went over and got the sack from the closet. I handed it to him. He put the bricks into it and wrapped it around so he could carry it under his arm.

"Okay," he said. "I'll talk to you tonight. Good luck."

"Thanks. I may need it."

I let him out and checked my watch. I had just about enough time. I quickly got ready, wrapped the rock from Ambrose's mine in newspapers, and went downstairs. I left a message with the desk clerk to let Mei into the room if she arrived before I did.

Then I went to meet a member of Angelo Bacci's family.

ELEVEN

I found Dino's Pub without any problem and parked the LTD a couple of doors from it. I went inside. It looked like dozens of other bars except that it was a little more fancy than the others. There were good paintings on the wall. There were a few small tables and booths in the back, although it was obvious they didn't serve food. There was a jukebox and three slot machines, and that was about all. There were several people sitting at the bar and one man sitting in a booth in the rear. I took a stool at the end of the bar. The bartender came over and stood in front of me.

"My name," I said, "is Milo March. I am supposed to meet Dino Mancetti here. In the meantime, I'll have an extra dry martini. Up."

He went back to mix the martini. I noticed that he looked toward the rear and nodded his head slightly. As he stirred the martini I put some money on the bar and waited, not showing any curiosity.

He brought the martini up and put it in front of me. "It's on the house," he said. "Mr. Mancetti will be with you in a few minutes."

I sipped at the drink and waited, making a point of not looking at the man who was sitting in the booth at the rear. I figured that had to be Mancetti, but there would be plenty of time to look at him later.

I drank slowly, but the martini was almost finished when the bartender strolled down to me again. "Mr. Mancetti will see you now," he said. "That's him in the booth back there. I'll make another martini for you."

I finished the one in front of me and walked toward the back of the bar. Even though he was sitting down, I could see he was a tall man. Tall and thin, with a grim face, as though life was a tough ordeal. I walked up to the booth.

"Mancetti?" I asked.

He nodded. "You're March?"

"I'm March. I was told that you wanted to talk to me."

He nodded. "Sit down. The bartender is bringing you a drink. After that we'll go have lunch."

I slipped into the booth opposite him, and the bartender arrived with my martini and another drink I didn't recognize. I lifted the martini. "Here's to crime."

His face darkened. "Look," he said angrily, "I don't know anything about crime. I'm a legitimate businessman. I own a whorehouse in a county where it's legal. I own this bar and I own a gold mine. Just because I'm Italian everyone thinks I'm a gangster. It's a lot of crap. I don't do nothing that's illegal. You're as bad as the newspapers."

"Don't get excited," I said. "I didn't say you were a gangster. I never saw you before. I couldn't say anything about you."

"Then why are you on my back?"

"I didn't know I was. You were the one who invited me here. I didn't invite you."

"You called my office and insisted on seeing me. Why?"

"I didn't insist on seeing you. I did insist on seeing your gold mine."

"Why should I show you my gold mine? I'm not interested in selling it. So I don't have to show it to anybody."

"No, you don't—now. I saw it last night after a man was killed by a trap that was set from your mine."

His face tightened and he was looking nervous. "I don't know anything about that. I haven't been in the mine since it was opened. I have two men who run it every day."

"I met one of them," I said dryly. "I read in the local paper about three men who were killed north of here. Were they your men, too?"

"I don't know what you're talking about," he said tightly.

"Of course not. Did you also know that a man named Angelo Bacci got in touch with me and told me to stop pushing you around?"

He was listening all right, but he was no longer staring at me. His gaze was fixed on the area around the front door. And he looked more uncertain than he had before.

"I never heard of him," he muttered.

"You will," I said cheerfully. "He's interested in what you do. Did you ever notice that he limps? Ask him who caused that."

I took a quick glance over my shoulder. There was a big, heavyset man walking toward us. He looked like a cop.

"What do you mean?" Mancetti said.

"I caused the limp. I've shot him twice. Once in Las Vegas, where he ended up in a prison hospital. Once in Miami Beach, where he ended up in an ordinary hospital. He beat the prison rap. The third time I may be lucky."

He was still staring past me. He licked his lips nervously. I glanced around. The man had arrived at the booth. He was only looking at Mancetti.

"Hello, Dino," he said.

"Hello, Bob," Mancetti said. "Sit down and have a drink."

"I'm on duty. Who's your friend?"

"Ask him."

The cop finally looked at me. "Who are you ... friend?"

"I'm very careful," I said evenly, "about giving my name to anyone who asks. There are so many perverts around these days—"

His face darkened slightly. "I'm Detective Sergeant Robert Mason of the Reno Police Department. Would you like to answer my question or would you prefer to go into the station and answer it?"

"I don't mind answering it, Sergeant. My name is Milo March. I represent the Intercontinental Insurance Company of New York. I am here on business. With Mr. Mancetti. I'm not sure that he has any friends, but if he does I'm not one of them."

"You're carrying a piece," he said.

"I am. I am also carrying a license for it which is good anywhere in the state of Nevada. Would you like to see it?"

"I would, but move slowly."

I reached into my pocket and brought out my ID folder. I flipped it open. My insurance card was in one window and my gun permit in the opposite one. I pushed it across the table. He picked it up and looked at it. Then he shoved it back to me.

"Okay," he said. "What are you doing with this punk?"

"Leaning on him," I said with a smile. "I wanted some answers to a few questions. You seem to have interrupted the answers."

"You might get a chance to ask them later." He looked at Mancetti. "Come on, Dino. We're going to the station."

"What's the beef?" Mancetti asked.

"There's two of them. One from the sheriff's office and the other from the Feds. Let's go, Dino."

Mancetti stood up and tried to look like a victim. "What's the charge?" he asked.

"No charge. We just want to ask you a few questions." He glanced down at me. "If you want to talk to him, you'll have to come down and see him in the cooler. He'll have a private room. We wouldn't throw an important man like him into a tank. We're very considerate."

"I'm sure," I said. "Sorry we didn't get to finish our conversation, Dino. I'll see you later."

He told me what I could do to myself. It wasn't very polite, so I ignored it. Never take advice from strangers.

"Don't you," I asked the cop, "have some kind of law against the use of obscenity in a public place?"

"If we have to," he said with a grin, "I imagine we can dig one up. But I think we have enough on him anyway. Let's go, Dino."

The two of them walked out. I reached down and picked up my drink. I left a dollar for the bartender and walked out.

I had been cheated out of my invitation to lunch, so I decided I'd better have something before I headed south.

I drove up and parked in the lot between First and Second on Sierra. I headed for the Waldorf. I was almost there when I recognized the man coming toward me. It was Manfred Smith, the assayer.

"Hello, Mr. Smith," I said.

He stopped and stared at me. But then his eyes began to focus. "Oh, hello," he said. "You're the—oh, yes—the man from the insurance company, aren't you? March, isn't it?"

"Yes, on both counts. I'm from the insurance company and my name is March."

"Were you coming to see me?"

"No. I was thinking of having lunch at the Waldorf. I will buy you a drink if you'd care to join me that long."

"No. No, I have to meet a client. Very important. I trust that everything is going well with your work here. Have you managed to see Mr. Mancetti?"

"I've seen him," I said. "We didn't get to talk long. He was arrested."

"Oh? Well, I suppose if you run an establishment like he does, you have to expect that once in a while."

"I guess so. Well, I don't want to keep you from your luncheon engagement. With a client."

"Of course, of course." He didn't sound as if he was quite tuned in on anything. "I hope that your talk, as brief as it may have been, was helpful to your cause. Did you have him arrested?"

"No. I believe it was the FBI."

"I see. Well, I must hurry on to meet my client. I hope that everything turns out well for you."

"It will," I said firmly. "It was nice seeing you again, Mr. Smith."

He nodded abruptly and scurried past me. I turned around and watched him. At the corner of First and Virginia, he stepped to the curb and hailed a taxi. I turned and went on to the Waldorf.

Joe saw me coming in and mixed a drink. He brought it up to me. "You're still here," he said. "I thought you would have finished all your work and been gone by now."

"It's almost finished," I said. "I think it will be by tomorrow. Just in time, too."

"Why just in time?"

"My girl is arriving tonight from Hong Kong. She's liable to get restless if I work all the time she's around."

"I can understand that," he said. "What does she do in Hong Kong?"

"She's a pirate."

He laughed. "Aren't they all?"

"But she is. Her father was one of the most successful river pirates, and she inherited the business. I think she's doing better than the old man did."

"You're kidding!"

"No. That's what she does. Her father worked the rivers. She mostly raids the mainland."

"Chinese?"

"Yes."

He laughed. "Is it true what they say about Chinese girls?"

"You know something?" I said. "Every time I could have checked on that, I was occupied with other things."

"I'll bet. Have you met Dino yet?"

"Yeah. Today but not for long. The cops picked him up."

For what? Dirty toilets at the Palomino Mare?"

"Maybe. The cop just said for questioning."

More customers came in and Joe went off to wait on them. I sipped on my drink. I heard the door open as someone else came in. I looked around. It was Carol Chilton. She looked a little upset.

"Hello," I said. "Come on over. We'll have the doctor mix up a little prescription for you."

She came over and sat on the stool next to me. "I think I can use one. Thank you."

Joe saw her and mixed a martini and brought it up. I shoved money in his direction and he went away. "Who's minding the store?" I asked.

"What do you mean?"

"I just saw Mr. Smith on the street as he was hurrying to meet a client."

"Sure," she said. "Will you tell me something, Milo? Is he in trouble?"

"What do you mean by trouble?"

"You know what I mean," she said. "He's been very nervous since you were up at the office."

"He's in trouble," I admitted.

"What kind of trouble?"

"Do you know who Dino Mancetti is?"

"I only know some things I've heard and that he is sometimes a client of Mr. Smith's. What does he have to do with this?"

"I don't know, honey. But he was arrested today. Less than an hour ago. Now, enough answers for you. Suppose you give me some answers, starting with the reason you're asking all these questions."

She gulped her martini and took a deep breath. "He got a phone call this morning. I don't know who it was, but I recognized the voice as someone who often calls him. He has a lot of legal friends who call and give him hints on business and things like that. But this one upset him. He came out a little later and told me he had to go out of town to see a client and he gave me a check. I didn't look at it until he was gone. It was for two weeks' wages. Does this have anything to do with Mr. Mancetti?"

"I'm sure it does. Have you cashed the check yet?"

"Yes. Then because the whole thing was very unusual, I asked the teller to give me the balance on his checking account. After cashing my check, it was only ten dollars. What does it mean?"

"I would guess that it means that your Mr. Smith has taken flight. It probably means that his other bank accounts may be depleted. I think it also means that you should start looking for another job. I imagine that you are a very efficient young lady, in addition to being a very attractive one, so you shouldn't have too much trouble getting one. I also suggest that you avoid employers who may suggest that you offer your fair, white body in exchange for information. You might take this advice as coming from a lay specialist."

She stood up and looked at me, her eyes big and round. Her face had tightened. "Shit!" she said suddenly.

"Honey," I said, "I couldn't have summed it up better myself."

I don't know if she heard me because she turned and was suddenly gone. I turned back and motioned for Joe to bring me another drink. He mixed it right away and came up with it.

"What was wrong with her?" he asked.

"It means that she has just discovered that she's been screwed, and I don't mean in the more socially acceptable manner. Her employer has deserted her and fled the scene."

"Smith?"

"The same. Now he can change his name to Jones and nobody will suspect it used to be Smith. And I suspect he has friends here who will let him know when the heat has died down and he might be able to come back. He's not too important to the case, so he may end up all right."

"Your case?"

"My case. Dino Mancetti was arrested not long ago, and I imagine others were at the same time. Dino had a very interesting idea, but he just wasn't big enough to carry it. Maybe whenever he gets out of this he'll stick to whorehouses. That's more his speed."

"So your case is finished?"

"In a manner of speaking. There's a couple of things that still have to be cleaned up. But within twenty-four hours I should be able to shake the dust of Nevada from my feet and head for New York."

"You and the Chinese broad?"

"Me and the Chinese broad. But go easy how you talk about her. Don't forget that she's also a lady pirate."

"I'll keep it in mind."

"While you're doing that, I'm going to go back and have lunch. Then I'll see what other damage I can do in this lovely little town. I may see you on the way out."

I picked up my glass and marched back to the restaurant. I took the first table on the left and ordered a hot turkey sandwich. It came right away and I went to work on it. I didn't linger afterwards. I left and went to the nearest casino-hotel and found a public stenographer and dictated a document. I asked her to make four copies and said I'd pick them up the next morning. I went and rescued the LTD from the parking lot and drove straight to Virginia City.

It's a small town. Apart from private homes, it consists almost entirely of bars and gambling places, souvenir shops, gun shops, and gold assayers.

I picked out one that seemed to be a combination and went in with my newspaper-wrapped bundle. I had to shift from foot to foot for a while before a man appeared from the inner caverns.

"Hello," he said. "Interested in guns?"

"No," I said. "I already have a gun, and I've never learned to shoot with my left hand. Are you an assayer?"

"Yes. Gold or silver."

"I want a report on a sample which I have here. I would like to have it as soon as possible. When could that be?"

"Depends," he said. He wasn't going to waste any words. "At the moment I ain't busy. We don't get much of that kind of business these days. But if a lot of people don't come in wanting to look at the old guns and not wanting to buy, or come in looking for souvenirs, I might get it done today. Where's the specimen?"

"Right here." I put it on his counter and unwrapped the paper. "Is that large enough?"

"Depends on what you mean by large enough. I can tell you the percentage of gold in that rock. As for the whole mine, it depends on how far the streak of gold runs. Ain't no way I can tell that without spending a day or more in the mine. There ain't many miracles around—especially these days."

"I stopped looking for miracles when I was ten years old," I said. "This comes from a mine owned by a friend of mine. He's been digging out enough gold to support himself and a friend of his. This is a different vein than he's been digging. I'm aware that it might run out at any minute. I'd like to know what it could be worth—if it's a long vein. That's all."

"Okay. You're in a hurry for it?"

"Sort of. I'm from New York City and I think I have to go back there tomorrow. I'd like to know the answer on this one chunk of rock by tonight or tomorrow morning."

"Ain't very busy. Ought to be able to tell you by tonight. Tell me where to reach you and I'll phone you."

"I'm at the Pony Express Hotel in Reno. The name's Milo March. I'll be there for certain between five and six tonight. I'll drop back down before I leave Reno to pick up the specimen and pay your bill."

"Fair enough," he said.

"There's something I'm curious about," I said. "What's that black rock partly around the gold?"

"Black magnetite. It's a heavy mineral but not especially valuable. It's often found with gold."

"Okay. That satisfies my curiosity. We'll talk tonight and I'll see you tomorrow."

I left and drove straight back to Reno. I was a little early, so I didn't stop at the hotel. I drove on up to Ambrose's house. The truck was parked beside it, so he was there. I parked and went up and knocked on the door.

"Who's there?" he called out.

"Milo," I said.

"Door ain't locked. Come on in."

I opened the door and stepped inside. He was sitting in a chair, just staring at the floor. He looked as if he hadn't even slept.

"Just stopped by to see how you are," I said.

"I feel a mite peaked," he said. "Can't seem to get anything done. You know, I miss that little cuss. Sit down and I'll get you a drink."

"I'll fix it," I said. "Do you want one, Ambrose?"

"Might as well, I guess. I think you'll find ice cubes in the refrigerator."

I went into the kitchen. The only glasses were dirty so I washed them. There were plenty of ice cubes and the bottle of bourbon was on the sink, still in the paper bag. I poured two drinks and carried them back inside.

"Did you get any rest today?" I asked.

"I got a few winks but didn't need no more."

"What about food?"

"Ain't been hungry."

"You have to eat something, Ambrose. Is there any food in the house?"

"There's all them sandwiches you brought last night. If I get hungry I can eat them."

"What have you been doing? Just sitting here?"

He nodded. "Sitting and thinking about Necktie. You know, I used to cuss him out and get mad at him, but I guess he was the only friend I had in the last forty years. I'm going to miss the little rascal."

"I know you will," I said. "I knew him for only a couple of days, but I think I'll miss him, too. It won't help much, but you may like to know that Dino Mancetti is in jail, and I think the two men who were his partners are, too."

"No, it won't bring Necktie back. But I hope they get strung up for doing what they did. I should've stopped Necktie when he started to go look at the bushes."

"In the first place, neither of us believed that there was a hole between the two mines. And we had no way of knowing that there was a trap in there. What are you going to do now, Ambrose?"

"Ain't thought none about it. Reckon I have to go on digging enough gold to keep body and soul together. Ain't nothing else to do, but I won't have to work too hard. There'll be only me to feed now."

"Do you have any relatives around?" I asked.

"Not much. I got a half brother a couple or three years younger than me. Last I heard he was living in Fallon. Don't rightly know if he's still there or even alive. That would be about all, I reckon."

"What about Necktie? Did he have any family around here?"

"Not here nor anywhere else."

"What does your half brother do?"

"Don't rightly know," he said. "Last I knew he was working for the post office. Reckon by now he might be retired."

"Any family?"

"His wife died several years ago, I heard. He maybe got married again, but I never heard anything about it. He had a couple of boys. Guess they must be men by now."

"Why don't you look them up?"

"No reason to, I guess. Twenty years is a long time."

"Did you like him?"

"He was all right. We just was never close. He used to josh me about being named after Ambrose Bierce, but that didn't bother me none. We just went different ways."

"If I were you," I said, "I'd look him up after a few days. You're going to need someone to help you work your mine, and if your brother has spent his life in the post office, he might get excited by the idea of doing some mining."

"He must get a pretty good pension," Ambrose said uncertainly.

"Anyone can always use a few extra dollars. But the world is full of people who wish they'd had a chance to dig gold. He might get ten years younger overnight. And if he's all alone, you both might get a lot of fun out of him living here with you."

He looked up, and for the first time his eyes had a little expression in them. "You know," he said, "that might be a good idea you have. I never thought of it that way. He just might be sitting around wishing he had something to do. And most people do get kind of excited about the idea of digging gold out of the ground. That's a pretty good head you got on your shoulders, Milo."

"It keeps my ears apart," I said. "There's something else I want you to do."

"What?"

"What was the name of that bar where I first met you? The Tun? Meet me there tomorrow about noon. I may have something else that will interest you."

"I'll be there," he said.

I stood up and finished my drink. "Get some sleep tonight," I said. "Finish the bottle if that's what it takes. I'll see you tomorrow. Good night, Ambrose."

"Good night," he muttered as I opened the door and went out.

As I drove away, I checked the time again. I still had a little leeway on getting back to the hotel, and another thought about the case had occurred to me. Dino and his two men were in jail, but he would have a lot of pressure on him. There was one thing that was strictly a guess, but I was certain I was right. Three men had been killed. But if there had been an around-the-clock guard on the place where the gold had been stored, then there should be another six men not accounted for and probably not dead. That could mean they had sold out to Dino.

That, in turn, could mean something else. Dino must suspect that his plan to steal the rest of the Syndicate gold was in danger. He would know that he would have to move all the remaining gold as quickly as possible. He wouldn't wait until he got out of jail. He would get word to someone to move it quickly. They might not even wait until it was dark. He would be able to make a phone call, and that was all that would be needed.

I cut to the left and drove until I reached Virginia Street, then swung left again. It was a short drive to the house where the truck had gone from Virginia City. Everything seemed quiet, but there was a truck parked right next to a hill below the house. I made a sharp turn on a narrow road. Just ahead of me there was another dirt road leading up into the hills. I took it, ending up on a little mesa which gave a clear view of the main road below. I parked there and waited.

Finally a door opened in what I'd thought was just a hill, and two men came out and got into the truck. They drove a few feet away and waited. Then a second truck drove right out of the hill and a door flipped down. Things were getting interesting. I started the motor of my car and waited.

The two trucks stood side by side for a minute, and it looked as if the two drivers were talking to each other. Finally one of them pulled ahead and turned toward Reno when he reached the highway. The other one followed and turned in the opposite direction. I had a good idea where the first one was going, so I turned my car around and drove quickly down to the highway and turned to follow the second truck.

Within a few minutes I was in sight of it. I slowed up and stayed at some distance behind. A car passed me and dropped in between us. That suited me fine, so I merely cruised along and watched. I had checked the mileage, and after almost three miles the truck turned into a road angling off from the highway. When I reached it, I turned and followed the truck.

We drove for about four miles, and then the truck made a left turn into a dirt road leading to what looked like a farmhouse and barn. But it was practically all desert there, so I doubted if there could be much farming. The house also looked better than most houses on farms. More like the house of someone who wanted to live out in the country but worked in the city. As I went by, the truck had turned and was backing up to the barn. I went on past it.

Just past it, there was a slight curve in the road, and there was a private road leading up a small hill to the right. I used it to turn around.

As I drove past the barn where the truck was parked, there were two men unloading boxes from the truck and carrying them into the barn. It was obvious that the boxes were very heavy. Heavy like gold. I decided I'd seen enough and turned left toward Reno when I reached the highway.

I drove straight to the Pony Express Hotel and parked in the lot. It was a few minutes before five. I went inside and picked up a Reno city map from a display of free maps by the entrance. I went on to the desk.

"March," I said to the clerk. "Any messages for me?"

He looked at the boxes. "No," he said, "but Mrs. March arrived a few minutes ago. She's upstairs."

"Thank you," I said. So she had gotten there earlier than she had said she would. I took the elevator up and walked to the room. I unlocked the door gently and opened it slightly.

I could hear the shower running as I stepped inside. I closed the door behind me.

I took off my jacket and hung it up in the closet. There was still a little bit of gin and orange juice left, so I made myself a drink. I sat down on the edge of the bed and kicked my shoes off. I lit a cigarette and took a swallow of the drink. It tasted fine even without ice in it. Then I picked up the phone and in a quiet voice ordered two dry martinis. I leaned back and relaxed.

The shower stopped running and I could hear her humming in the bathroom. I smiled and waited.

The bathroom door opened. Then, still humming, she came out. She had a robe in her hand but that was all. It was the way it should be. There is no way to improve on the natural beauty of a naked woman.

"I'm glad I came early," I said. "As the poet Yuan Mei once wrote: 'Late in the day the flowers are not at their best.'* But now you look beautiful. Your body is as lovely as the most precious *ke yu*." That was the name of the most valuable Chinese jade.

"Milo," she said, her face lighting up. "How did you get here?"

"You're forgetting that I temporarily live here and so have a key. You might at least come and give me a kiss."

She dropped her robe and came to the bed. She gave me a long, warm kiss that was more than a welcome. Then she straightened up. But before she could say anything, there was a knock on the door.

"Who's that?" she asked, startled.

* Yuan Mei was a great 18th-century Zen poet. This line is taken from Arthur Waley's translation of a fairly straightforward poem about the poet's wonderful garden, in which he urges an invited guest to come early.

"I imagine it's room service," I said. "I ordered two martinis while you were still in the bathroom. Now you can put on your robe, let the waiter in, and sign the check or you can hide in the bathroom. It wouldn't do to open the door as you are now. The martinis would drop on the floor and the poor man would probably never be the same again."

She turned and darted into the bathroom without picking up the robe. I walked over and let the waiter in. He carried the martinis over to the table and put them down. I added a tip to the check and signed it. He left, pretending not to see the robe on the floor.

"You can come out," I called. I partly opened the drapes over the window beside the table. There was a lovely view overlooking a part of the city and, beyond that, the mountains. I crossed back to the door and hung the *Do Not Disturb* sign on the outside knob.

"You can come out, honey," I said.

I heard the bathroom door open as I walked past but I continued on to the table before looking back. She was walking uncertainly toward me. "Shouldn't you close the drapes?" she asked.

"No. There's a nice view. Nobody can see into the room unless they're in a low-flying plane. Come on."

She peered out the window and then sat down. She stared out the window. "It is lovely." She glanced at me. "Aren't you uncomfortable in those stuffy-looking clothes?"

I smiled and went across the room. I undressed and put my clothes in the closet. I took my cigarettes and lighter from my jacket and went back to the table.

"Better?"

"Oh, yes," she said. She reached out and touched me softly. "It's been so long I had almost forgotten what you looked like."

"I didn't forget what you looked like," I said with a smile. "Are you going to take the rest of the day to finish that martini?"

"Why? Are we going somewhere?"

"Darling, last night was a very long day, and the same has been true of today. And tonight I—which means we—have to go out again in about two hours." I picked up my martini. "There's an old toast which you must remember from Smith College. Down the hatch."

We both finished our martinis. She stood up and walked slowly across to the bed. It was a beautiful sight.

I went over and stretched out on the bed next to her. She came into my arms. "It really has been a long time, Milo," she said.

She was right. It had been a very long time.

TWELVE

The telephone awakened me. I opened my eyes, but it was still a few seconds before I realized where I was and what was happening. The phone rang again. I swung my legs off the bed and sat up, suddenly aware that Mei was curled up next to me. I picked up the phone receiver and answered.

"Mr. March?" a man's voice asked.

"Yes."

"This is the gold assayer in Virginia City. I finished examining that specimen you left with me. Of course, I can only report on what you left with me. The specimen is very rich with gold. If there is a vein like this which runs any distance, then you have a valuable mine."

"Thank you," I said. "I'll be down in the morning to pick up the report and to pay you. What time are you open in the morning?"

"Nine o'clock."

"I'll be there shortly after that. Thanks." I hung up and walked over to the table by the window. There was still a little gin and a little orange juice. I looked over at Mei. She was awake, staring at me with her big, dark eyes.

"Good morning, darling," she said.

"It's not morning. I can offer you a gin and orange juice without ice or we can call room service."

"Don't call room service," she said. "I don't want to get dressed. I'm too comfortable."

I poured the two drinks and walked back to the bed. I handed one to her and sat down on the edge of the bed. The phone rang again. I answered it.

"Milo?" he said. "Frank. Anything?"

"Yes. Where are you?"

"In the hotel."

"Give us thirty minutes and then come up."

"Us?"

"Yeah. I want you to meet a real, live lady pirate. It'll give you a story to tell the boys back in the Bureau on cold winter nights."

"Okay," he said and hung up.

I looked at Mei. "I guess you have to get dressed even if you don't feel like it. In thirty minutes, there will be a nice Federal Bureau of Investigation agent here to talk to me. We must present some decorum."

She sat up and said a dirty word in Chinese. "And what was that bit about a lady pirate?"

"Well, you are. It should thrill him. And you don't have to worry. You don't operate in this country. Or have you expanded?"

"Why is he coming up here? Are you in trouble?"

"No. He's coming for some information which I want to give him. No problems. Now, run to the bathroom. I have to get ready, too."

She made a face at me and slid off the bed and headed for the bathroom. I got up and walked over to the table and picked up my cigarettes, then went back and sat down. I lit a cigarette and sipped my drink. I could hear the shower running, so I relaxed and thought about what was coming next.

She was out in fifteen minutes, wearing a red and yellow Chinese robe. "There!" she said triumphantly.

"You look lovely," I told her. "And in such a short time, too. What are you wearing under that robe?"

"Why don't you try to find out?"

"You're cheating," I said. "You know that I don't interfere with your work when I'm in Hong Kong. If I'm not out of the shower in ten minutes, call room service and order three dry martinis."

I was out of the shower just as she hung up after ordering the drinks. I got dressed in time to even light a cigarette before the knock came on the door. I went over and let the waiter in. I signed the check while he was putting the drinks on the table and shooed him out. But he was barely gone before there was another knock on the door and I let Frank in.

Mei," I said, "I'd like you to meet Frank Newton. He's a cop but a good one. Frank, this is Mei Hsu, my own private lady pirate."

"I only heard the lady part," he said. "Hello, Miss Hsu. Welcome to America."

"Thank you," she said, "but I've been here before. I graduated from Smith College. A long time ago."

"It doesn't look like it was so long ago." He looked at me. "We can talk?"

"If everybody sits down, one in front of each martini."

He smiled. "I'm really on duty and I'm not supposed to drink."

"Nonsense. You're not on duty. You're consorting with the enemy, a private detective and a beautiful lady pirate. I doubt if that's legal either, so you might as well go the whole route. They can only hang you once."

He laughed. "If anyone were listening, I doubt that the distinction would be appreciated. Besides, we don't have any hanging judges in these modern times."

"That's the trouble with FBI agents," I said to Mei. "They always have to prove that they're educated. I doubt if more than a dozen of them ever heard of Judge Roy Bean, the hanging judge.* We have a lot of hanging judges today, but they are usually called jurists, which everyone feels makes us superior to the more primitive American past. After all, we no longer hang small children for stealing a loaf of bread when they're hungry. Which proves we have progressed, although it is a distinction that the hangee might have trouble with."

"All right," he said, "what's the story?"

"I haven't written the script yet. What do you have?"

"The gold bars were stolen from an operating mine in California. That's about all we know about them. The rest is your department."

"Do you have your little battalion of men?"

"Yes."

"How many?"

"Nine. I can get more in less than two hours if needed."

---

* The legendary judge was an eccentric saloonkeeper and justice of the peace in southwestern Texas in the late18th–early 19th century. Despite his nickname, he only hanged two men.

"Good." I got up and walked to the closet. I took the map and a pencil from my jacket and went back to the table. I spread the map and found the spot I was looking for. I marked it with the pencil.

"This is where they've been keeping the gold. This afternoon two trucks left there, I imagine with gold. One went south and the other north and then east. I followed the second truck. It turned here and drove a few miles to an area which is between hills and desert. It stopped there. Heavy boxes were unloaded and taken into a barn. You can bet they contained gold. It's a very attractive house and barn just below the road to the left. I don't know if anyone lives there, but you can be sure there'll be a guard somewhere."

"The other truck?" he asked.

"I don't know since I didn't follow it. But I think it had to be going to the New Yukon Mine just west of Virginia City on the road to Carson City. I doubt if the gold has all been removed yet, and there will probably be more moved tonight and tomorrow. I would like to suggest that you have all three spots guarded, starting tonight. I doubt if there will be any crucial action until after Dino and his two friends get out of jail tomorrow. They will be held until then, won't they?"

"Yes. They will have the charges made against them by noon tomorrow at the latest. Then they can get bail, which I'm sure that they will. Do you mind telling me what you will be doing?"

"Not at all," I said ignoring his sarcasm. I looked at my watch. "In a very few minutes, I will call Bacci and arrange to see him briefly tonight. I don't think he will do anything before tomorrow about the information which I will give him, but your men should be present just in case."

"Mr. Newton," Mei said, "do you always let Milo tell you what to do?"

He smiled at her. "I don't let him tell me what to do at any time. But he does have information, and we take that from wherever we can get it. I know pretty much what he has in mind, which I'm sure is quite illegal, but he is also the only person who could probably set this up. Go ahead, Milo."

"It's simple," I said. "Bacci is undoubtedly here to check on the operation Dino is carrying on for the Syndicate. I imagine that he has suspicions of what Dino is trying to do. But he needs help. I doubt if he can get it before tomorrow, so he won't move until then. Dino must have found a way to get to six of the nine men who were assigned to help him. I think that Bacci has only one gunman with him at the moment, but he should get the others he needs quickly. Bacci himself will go along with them when they move. He has that sort of ego."

Frank nodded. "What's next?"

"Tomorrow morning I go to the jail to see Dino and his two friends. Today I dictated a quitclaim paper to a public stenographer. It will be typed up and I'll take it with me and have them sign it. That will take Intercontinental off the hook and my charges will be dropped. You'll still be able to charge them with possession of stolen property. While we're on that subject, why don't you have a deposition drawn up covering my finding the gold bars on the property presently owned by Dino's company and I will sign it. Be sure to date it as of today. I expect to be finished with my business tomorrow, and Mei and I will leave as quickly as we can."

"What about the murder charge? Aren't you a witness to that?"

"Not really. The only thing I could swear to is that I heard someone scream and that we found the body. The sheriff's office also found the body, in the same condition and position as Ambrose Fenner and I found it. I don't think they'll get a murder one. I think the best they can get is involuntary manslaughter, and I doubt if they can make that stick. The snare was set on Dino's property and Necktie's head was across the property line, so legally he was a trespasser. Once they have examined what they have, I doubt if they will even prosecute. For your needs, you have enough."

"I think so," Frank said. "We'll have conspiracy to steal the gold from the mining company in California, conspiracy to transport stolen property across state lines, possession of stolen property, and the sale of same. From what you've told me and what you've given me, there should be no difficulty getting a conviction. If necessary, you'll come back for a trial?"

"Sure. I'd rather not, but I will if needed. One more thing, Frank. There is another person who at the very least is an accessory after the fact. He's Manfred Smith, an attorney and assayer. You'll find him listed in Reno, but he's already jumped town. I don't know where you can find him, but I'd bet that if you do, he will be a witness for the prosecution."

"Okay." He gathered up the map and his notes. "When will I hear from you?"

"As soon as I finish talking to Bacci. Say two hours from now. Where will you be?"

"Here. I can get the coverage for tonight set up by that time. I'll wait for your call." He turned to Mei. "It was nice to meet you, Miss Hsu. Even if you are what he calls a lady pirate, I think I should warn you that you are consorting with a man who has criminal inclinations and ability. You should be careful." He smiled as he finished.

"I shall be," she said gravely. "Fortunately, he is not inscrutable. Thank you, Mr. Newton."

"You are welcome, Miss Hsu. By the way, I understand that you brought some property with you into the country. I have checked and it is all perfectly legal."

"I wasn't worried," she said calmly. "But thank you."

He nodded and left.

"What was that all about?" I asked when he was gone.

"About some property of mine," she said. "What was all that nonsense about seeing someone tonight? I thought you were taking me out tonight."

"I am. But I am also leaving you for a few minutes to see a man—as you heard."

"If you walk out of that door without me, I shall take off this robe, open the door, and start screaming as loud as I can."

"That," I said, "would be better than the *Late, Late Show.* But that isn't what I had in mind."

"What did you have in mind?"

"If you will stop yapping like a Chinese yenta, I will tell you. If you will also go get dressed—quickly—you and I will leave this hotel and descend to the lower depths of Reno. We will go to one of the larger casinos and I will leave you to the tender mercies of the gambling tables while I see the man. Then I will return and drag you away from your vice and we will have dinner. After that, we shall return to the hotel and make love—with a certain amount of time for sleep since tomorrow is another working day."

"Under those circumstances, I will get dressed." She removed the robe, tossed it over the back of the chair, kissed me on the cheek before I could react, and was gone into the bathroom. I lit a cigarette and leaned back, thinking of the next step.

She didn't take long. When she came out, she looked lovely. "Why aren't you ready?"

"I am except for a jacket." I took the jacket from the closet and put it on. "Aren't you going to wear something else?"

"Should I?"

"Something light. The nights get a little cooler."

She moved past me and reached into the same closet. She pulled out a mink jacket. As she slipped into it, she looked at me. "You're not wearing a tie."

"How observant of you. I thought you knew I was the casual type."

"Too casual, sometimes. Ready?"

"After you." I opened the door and held it for her. As she went through, I gave her a friendly pat on the bottom and followed her.

"My father was right," she said, as I closed the door. "He always told me that you Occidentals would only want me for my exotic looks."

"That's no Occident," I said. "Besides, it was you who first seduced me."

"Only because I was quicker than you. Where are we going?"

"You'll find out when we get there. Come on."

We went downstairs and out the back. I put my hand on her elbow and exerted pressure in the direction we were going. "I have a rented car over here."

"No," she said firmly. "We're going in the opposite direction. I have something to show you."

We walked along a row of parked cars. Then, suddenly, ahead I saw a car that looked out of place even there. It was a gleaming new Cadillac, the largest they make. It made every other car on the lot look like a compact.

"I wonder who that belongs to," I said innocently.

"You," she said.

I glanced at the license plate and saw "Hong Kong."

"I thought you flew over."

"I did. And so did the car. It's my present to you. Here is the proof of ownership and here are the keys. It is custom-made and has many special features which I will show you later when we have more time. But there is a fully stocked bar in the back seat. There are clever little pockets in the front and the rear where you can conceal guns, and there are many other clever pockets where almost anything can be hidden. There are all kinds of special equipment built into it, which I will also explain later. And it is bulletproof."

"And gets two miles to the gallon," I said bitterly. "What the hell am I going to do with that in the middle of New York City? You ordered that made for me?"

"No. I was not so rash as that. The car was made on order for a man in Hong Kong who might have been called a modern river pirate. Unfortunately, he died unexpectedly the same day the car was delivered. I bought it from his estate at a very special price. I thought it would amuse you and you would be pleased."

"I am," I said halfheartedly. "I just don't know what the hell to do with it."

"I had thought that we might drive it from Reno to New York as a kind of holiday together. I drove it from Los Angeles here and it really drives very well. I could drive and you could sit in the back with the bar. There's also a television set."

"Don't tell me any more. I'm not sure I could stand it all at once. But we can't drive back. I don't have that much time. We'll have to have our holiday together in New York City. Let's get downtown."

"We can't drive your new car?"

"No. We'd get arrested if we even tried to park it. We'll drive down in the LTD. We'll worry about this one tomorrow. Let's go."

We drove down to the casino and turned the car over to an attendant to park and went inside. We stopped at one of the bars and I ordered two martinis. Mei was glancing around at all the action, and there was a look of excitement on her face.

"What are you going to play?" I asked.

"I think roulette or the dice table."

"Do you need any money?"

She looked surprised. "I don't think so. But how do I find the manager?"

"Why?"

"I know that most casinos here have a limit on how much you can bet. I want to have the limit removed in the event that I do want to bet more."

"How much do you have on you now? In cash."

"About twenty thousand dollars. I have some traveler's checks and I have bank accounts in San Francisco, New York, and Chicago. Then I have charge accounts."

"I shouldn't have asked," I said. "I imagine you'll have no trouble getting the limit raised. See one of the cashiers and tell her what you want, and there probably will be someone at your elbow before you've finished talking. I'll go make my phone call and hopefully see my man. When I come back, I'll see if I can locate you and then wait at this bar for you. Good luck, baby."

"I always have good luck. You will be gone long?"

"I don't think so. I'll also make a dinner reservation and we'll have dinner here. Slay 'em, tiger." I kissed her on the cheek and left. I didn't have to look back to know that she was heading for a table.

First I made a reservation. Then I got to a phone booth and made my call to Joseph Bottelli. I finally got through. "This is Milo March," I told the voice that answered. "Tell Angelo I would like to talk to him for a few minutes."

There was a moment of muffled conversation as he covered the phone with his hand, then he came back on. "He says to come on up."

I took the elevator to the top floor and rang the bell at the first suite. The door was opened by a tough-looking hood. "March?" he asked.

I nodded and he opened the door wider. I stepped inside. Bacci was sitting on the same sofa. He waved a hand. "Come on in, Milo. What do you want?"

"Hello, Angelo," I said. "I just dropped by because I wanted to tell you a story which I think might interest you."

"Is it about the case you said you were working on?"

"Not directly. Anyway, my case is finished. I'm just trying to do you a good turn."

I went over and sat down in the chair. I unbuttoned my jacket but left it on. "I see you got yourself a new boy."

"I got several new boys. What's your story?"

I waited until the hood at the bar brought over a martini. "I guess," I said, "it should start with 'once upon a time.' Anyway, let us say there was a group of businessmen. They got possession of some gold. Let us say that it was hot and therefore difficult to sell. In fact, impossible in the United States. It was in the form of gold bars, each one stamped with the symbol of the place from which it had come. Theoretically they could sell it here for thirty-five dollars an ounce, which would be all profit, but difficult to accomplish.* They could also sell it for sixty to seventy dollars an ounce in Hong Kong or India. But the problem would be how to get it there. In the first place, there were about a thousand tons of this gold and it would have to be transported to a shipping point."

"Well, there are planes and trucks."

"Out, I think, for several reasons. A thousand tons is a big load. Also, I suspect that the authorities knew it was some-

---

* The U.S. gold price had remained at $35 since 1934. In 1972 (probably after this manuscript was completed) the price was raised to $38 and in 1973 to $42.22.

where in this area. Moving it would have attracted attention. So it was stashed away and was guarded. An unimportant member of the group was appointed custodian of it. Then the situation changed. It became legal to sell gold to brokers in this country and the price went up to as high as seventy dollars. About then somebody had a bright idea. Why not buy an old gold mine and pretend there was still gold in it? I suspect the idea came from the custodian and he got himself cut in for a small percentage."

"What does this have to do with me?" he asked irritably.

"If you don't know, then I'm wasting my time trying to do you a favor. Do you want to hear more?"

"Go ahead."

"About this time, the custodian began to get greedy. It happens in the best of families. He wanted more than the percentage he was getting. I think he started to move some of the gold to another mine and sold it from there and kept all the money. In each mine, the hot gold was melted and then recast into new bricks with a new stamp on it. A smart idea. But the custodian became even greedier. He decided that he might take all of the gold."

Bacci was beginning to look more interested. "How would he do that?"

"Easy. There were, I think, nine guards watching the gold around the clock. They were well paid and they stayed out of Reno so that nobody knew about them. The custodian, let us say, had access to a supply of girls, who he provided for the guards. The girls and booze made them content to stay out of sight. Then the custodian got another bright idea. Why shouldn't he have all the gold? He discovered that six of the nine guards could be bought. That made it perfect. He bought them off and killed the other three. Then he could claim to his boss that the gold had been hijacked. And he began moving it to another location."

"Where?" Bacci was beginning to openly show his interest.

"If anyone knew where the gold was originally stored," I said, "all he would have to do is go exactly three miles past it where there is a road leading off to the right. He could go along that road for another four miles where there is a very nice-looking house and barn below the road on the left, and he would find all or most of the gold stored in the barn."

I finished the martini and stood up. "Well, I thought it might be an interesting story for you to tell the boys when you get back to Miami Beach. I'll see you around, Angelo." I headed for the door.

"Milo," he said.

I turned around. "Yes, Angelo?" I asked.

"Thanks. I won't forget this."

"I'm sure you won't," I said evenly. "Good night, Angelo." I walked out of the suite.

Down in the casino, I finally spotted Mei at the roulette table. As soon as she saw me, I turned and went to the bar. She joined me a few minutes later. I had already ordered a drink for her.

"How was your meeting?" she asked.

"Jolly," I said. "How was your shift in the salt mines?"

"Not bad. I think I won somewhere in the neighborhood of fifty-seven thousand dollars."

"That's a lovely neighborhood. I suppose you're carrying it in your little purse?"

"Yes."

"I suggest," I said, "that we finish our drinks and then we toddle over to the nearest cashier where you ask them to hold the money for you. They will give you a receipt for it and you can redeem it tomorrow. Then we can go eat dinner and after that to the hotel, where we will sink into beautiful sleep."

"Why leave the money here?"

"You surprise me, darling. You're supposed to be the sophisticated lady pirate from the wicked city of Hong Kong. Reno is a nice little city, but there are certain citizens who are fond of picking up extra money if they see it lying around. And tonight I feel like a lover, not a fighter."

"You just said the magic word," she said. She finished her drink. "Let's go, lover." So we went over to the cashier and she left sixty thousand dollars with the house and then we went to dinner. After that we went straight back to the hotel. I called Frank's room and he answered on the first ring.

"I saw Bacci," I said, "and told him about the fairy gold and the bad prince who was moving it. He was very interested. Do you have your men staked out?"

"At all three spots. No action yet."

"I doubt if Bacci will make a move until tomorrow. He's got a new man to replace the one who died so suddenly, but he'll need more than that. The nearest place he can get additional men is probably San Francisco, so it'll be tomorrow before he'll try anything. The place he'll go will obviously be the second one on your list. I gave him a good description of that."

"We'll be ready. What's your schedule for tomorrow?"

"I'm going to Virginia City early in the morning, then back to Reno. I want to see Dino in jail, where I hope he will sign a release on his claim for insurance money. That will complete my case. Then I have to see an old fellow who owns a gold mine. That's purely personal. Then we pack our little bags and catch a plane for New York. I should be back here at the hotel by one o'clock."

"I'll check with you then."

"May I make a suggestion, Frank?"

"Why not?" he asked dryly. "You've been making most of them so far."

"Why don't you file your additional charges against Dino and his two friends early in the morning? You've certainly got him on the possession charge and you might catch him on the other charges. If nothing else, they will push up the amount of the bail, although I doubt if Dino will be anxious to get out of jail."

"All right. I'll be at the hotel by one and will call you. I'll hate to see you leave town. I don't know what I'd do without you—although I'd like to find out."

"You'll think of something," I said dryly and hung up. I looked at Mei, who was watching me with amusement. "Let's go to bed, honey. It will be a busy day tomorrow."

While I was on the phone she had undressed. She was lying across the bed, a smile on her face. "You know," she said, "you haven't even asked me if I wanted to leave tomorrow. I had thought I might do some shopping here, but I guess there isn't much I could buy except cowboy boots and hats, and I'm not sure they would go well in Hong Kong. Tell me something, darling."

"What?"

"I've known you for several years now, and I've noticed your willingness to break almost any law if it was to your advantage, but you are suddenly very law-abiding. You are going out of your way to help your Federal police catch all kinds of people. What is the cause of this sudden virtue?"

"Because an old man died," I said simply. "An old man who never harmed anyone in his life. He never was a threat to anyone. But there was a hole between two mines and he was curious about what was on the other side of the hole. Anyone would have been curious. But he tried to crawl through the hole to find out for himself. A trap had been set like the kind a primitive hunter would use to catch an animal. The old man died, choked to death by a rope around his neck. And another old man felt like dying because his only friend had been killed for no reason. Does that answer your question?"

"Yes, Milo. Come to bed. You said that tomorrow will also be a tough day."

I got undressed and climbed into the bed. She snuggled up next to me. "Milo?" she said.

"Yes?"

"Why don't you marry me?"

"I've already told you, Mei. If I keep the job I have, and I probably will for the rest of my life, I would be gone half the time and you'd never know what was going to happen to me. It wouldn't be fair to you. And there is another side to it. I think it would be wonderful to be married to you, but there is no way of marrying you without also marrying your money. At the risk of being called a male chauvinist pig, I'd rather support you than have it the other way."

"I thought you knew our Chinese customs," she said. "If my father were alive, you would go to him and ask for my hand in marriage. He would then tell you what my dowry would be, and if you still wanted to marry me he'd probably give his consent. Since my father is no longer alive, I am head of the family of Hsu and so you may ask me."

"I should have known there was a trick to it. Forget it."

"In addition," she said, "my father would have offered you a position that would enable you to maintain your male ego. I do the same. You may work with the men who raid the mainland for me and be paid as they are. They all know of you and respect you. And you will be able to make more money than you do now."

"Really?" I said. "You know how long I have been here. I get three hundred dollars a day plus expenses, which is no small item, and tomorrow I expect to have a document which will guarantee that I will receive another twenty thousand dollars."

"If you can make that much money, then you don't need to know about the dowry. We can get married. In the meantime, with no money involved, would you consider making love to me?"

What could I say? I turned and took her in my arms.

It was seven-thirty in the morning when I awakened. That was just about the right time. I got out of bed and went into the bathroom. I had a fast shower, looked in the mirror, and decided that I might get by without shaving. I came out and got dressed. Then I looked down at Mei. She was still sound asleep. I sat down on the edge of the bed and gently stroked her stomach until she began to stir. Finally, her eyes opened.

"Good morning, darling," I said. "What would you like for breakfast?"

"Why?" she asked. I had to admit it was a sensible question.

"Because it's time for breakfast and I'm going to order it from room service. What would you like?"

"What do they have?"

"Another good question." I went over to the table and came back with the menu and handed it to her. She glanced at it sleepily.

"I guess scrambled eggs, Virginia ham, and hashed brown potatoes. Orange juice and coffee. White toast. That's all."

"I'm glad to see you haven't lost your appetite." I picked up the phone and ordered for both of us. Then I told them to send with it a bottle of gin, a large container of orange juice, and a bucket of ice. When the waiter arrived, he had a big smile on his face. I guess because he could figure out that with two of us, his tip should be twice as large.

"I'm going to Virginia City this morning," I said after breakfast. "Then I'm coming back to pay a short visit at the jail. After that I'm meeting an old prospector at a bar for a couple of drinks. Want to come along?"

"I'd like to," she said, "but I have a couple of things to do this morning. What time are we leaving?"

"I'll call the airline before I leave and find out. I imagine about two or three this afternoon. Do you want to call and make a reservation at a hotel in New York?"

She looked surprised. "I thought I would be staying at your apartment. Or is there someone else staying there?"

"Not that I know of. I like the idea. It's a nice apartment, but I didn't think you'd want to entertain your old Smith friends there."

"I'll only meet them for lunch and things like that. I'd rather spend most of my time with you."

"Good. I'll call about the plane right now and then we can plan our time."

I got a reservation for three that afternoon. "Okay, honey. We're booked for shortly after three. We fly to San Francisco and from there to New York. It'll get us there a little late, but we can sleep as long as we wish in the morning. Now I have to make certain of one more thing."

This time I put in a collect call to Martin Raymond at Intercontinental in New York. It didn't take him long to get on the phone.

"Milo, my boy," he exclaimed. I'd been demoted again. "Where are you?"

"Reno, Nevada. Remember that's where you sent me? A minor problem about two million dollars. I've saved you the two million and I've cost you twenty thousand dollars. Have the check for that and for the daily charge when I come in tomorrow morning. You can send me the expense money later. I'll drop in early tomorrow to pick up my two checks and then I'm taking a vacation. I trust you approve."

"Of course, my boy. The Board will be very pleased."

"I'm pleased that the Board will be pleased. If you run up the right flag, I might even salute it. See you tomorrow, Martin." I hung up.

When I turned around, Mei was smiling. "You know, I think that's the chief reason I liked you when I first met you at my father's house."

"What is?"

"You are an arrogant bastard, as we used to say at Smith. Will he really pay you twenty thousand dollars?"

"Of course. They're saving two million dollars. And I'm sure they received a handsome premium before they issued the policy, so they're still ahead. I have to say one thing for them. They may be stupid about issuing some policies, but they never are about the money they charge. Want to have lunch with me today?"

"Of course I do. Where and when?"

"There's a restaurant on Virginia Street between First and Second called the Waldorf. I'll meet you there about twelve. We'll have lunch and it will still give us an hour or so to clean up other things before we leave. Now there's one more thing."

"What?"

"I want to borrow ten thousand dollars until tomorrow."

She stood up and walked over to her purse, then solemnly counted out the money in hundreds.

"Thanks," I said. "Tomorrow morning I'll go to the bank and cash the check and bring you the ten big ones. And speaking of cash, may I make a suggestion?"

"You will, no matter what I say, so go ahead."

"When you pick up your money you left at the casino, have them give it to you as a check. It's safer in every way."

"All right, darling. Run along and I'll meet you for lunch."

I felt a little like I was being pushed out of my own room, but I left. I got into the LTD and drove straight to Virginia City. The assayer's store was open and I entered. The man came out from a back office.

"Good morning, Mr. March," he said. "I have the report and your specimen right here. As you'll read in the report, the specimen is very rich in gold. If the vein runs any distance at all, it should be very profitable. May I make a suggestion?"

"Sure," I said.

"If it's possible to do so, I would stake out claims on either side in the directions the vein seems to run. That will give you further protection."

I thanked him and paid him for the report. I took the specimen with me. I drove back to Reno, stopped by the public stenographer, and picked up the papers I had dictated. Then I drove to police headquarters. There was a young-looking sergeant on duty. I put my ID in front of him.

"As you can see," I said, "I work for Intercontinental Insurance, based in New York. I believe you are holding a Dino Mancetti here, and I would like permission to talk to him for a few minutes."

"What about?"

"We have a charge against him, but if he will sign a quitclaim, we'll drop our charges."

"What's a quitclaim?"

"He's trying to collect insurance from us on a policy which

was acquired by fraud. This is only to make sure that at a later date he doesn't start a suit against us."

"Let me see the papers."

I handed over the papers covering the quitclaim. He glanced at them. "I guess it's all right. You want to see the other two guys, too?"

"Yes. They're all officers and owners of the corporation which is involved."

"Okay. They ain't in the same cell but they are close together. You don't have to see them alone, do you?"

"No. All I need is their signatures. Then the charges will be dropped."

"There will be other charges made today."

"I know and I don't care about them. I believe that there will be additional Federal charges made before noon. I'm only interested in the one charge which concerns the insurance company."

"Okay. Go up that flight of stairs over there and knock on the door. I'll tell them you're coming." He picked up his phone as I headed for the stairs.

My knock was answered by a uniformed woman. "You're March?" she asked.

I admitted I was and she let me in, then led the way down the corridor and unlocked another door. "They're all three in there in different cells. When you're through, knock on this door and I'll let you out."

I stepped inside and she slammed the door behind me. It had an unpleasant sound. Dino was in the first cell. I walked up to it. He stared at me for a minute and then recognized me. "Hello, March," he said. "Did you have me thrown into the slammer?"

I shook my head. "I think it was the Federal cops and the sheriff's office. I can still file charges this morning, but if you sign these papers, I won't." I passed the papers through the bars. He looked at them.

"No insurance money?" he said.

"No insurance money. You know as well as I do that there hasn't been any gold in that mine in a hundred years until you started trucking the gold bricks in. You're not losing anything. Here's a pen." I passed it through the bars.

He signed the first papers. Then he looked at the second group. "What's this? I'm supposed to sign the mine over to you?"

"That's right. The mine isn't worth ten cents and you know it. Just sign it."

He did and passed the papers back to me. "Is that all?"

"Not quite. I want your two boys down the line to sign the papers, too. They're officers of your corporation."

He stared at me blankly for a minute, then shouted to Nick Lancer and Jerry Lake. I walked down to their cells. They both grumbled, but they signed. I walked back to Dino's cell. "I'm going to do you a favor, Dino. There will be some other charges filed against you within the next hour or so. Then you can put up bail to get out of here. I suggest that you don't."

"Why not?"

"You know Angelo Bacci is in town. He is already suspicious that the gold has been moved. It won't take him long to find out that it has. You'll be a lot safer in here. Sit it out and you might still be alive. Angelo is getting some guns from San Francisco."

His face paled as he looked at me. "Thanks a lot," he said bitterly.

I nodded and walked back to the door and knocked on it. The lady cop let me out. I reached in my pocket and pulled out three envelopes I had prepared the day before. They were addressed to the three men in the cells, and inside of each one there was a dollar bill, the amount of money for the transfer of the mine mentioned in the papers they had signed. I explained them to the lady and left.

I went back to the LTD and drove down Virginia to the bar that was known as the Tun. Don was on duty. I sat down and ordered a gin and orange juice.

Ambrose arrived in about thirty minutes. He looked much better than he had the day before. I ordered a bourbon for him.

"You know what?" he said. "I called my brother this morning. He'll be here this afternoon. He was very excited."

"I'm glad," I said. "I have some news for you, too. You know that stretch of black rock in the back wall of the second chamber of your mine?"

"What about it?"

"When you went to phone the sheriff night before last, I got curious about that. I dug out a chunk of it and took it to an assayer in Virginia City. Here's the report." I took the slip of paper from my pocket and passed it to him. He read it and then looked at me.

"But that's not the vein I've been working," he said.

"That's right," I said. "It's a different vein. The assayer

suggested that the property on each side of the vein be claim-staked."

"That makes sense," he said, "but it can only be done on one side. The other side is owned by Dino and his people."

"Not anymore." I took the other paper from my pocket and scribbled on it. "Now it's owned by you."

"I don't understand."

"You don't have to. Just record your claim. Do you have a bank account, Ambrose?"

"A small checking account at the First National Bank of Nevada."

"That's enough. Finish your drink and let's go."

"Where?"

"I'll tell you later. Come on."

He tossed down the drink. "I don't understand."

"You will," I said. "Let's go." I motioned to Don and he came over. I pushed some bills over. "That's for the drinks with something left over for you. I found your hidden gold."

"What?"

"I'll tell you some other time. I have a tight schedule. I'll tell you the next time around."

Ambrose and I left. When we were outside I noticed he had his truck parked there. I told him I'd meet him at his bank.

I got in the LTD and left. I was in luck. I found a place to park right in front of the bank and went in. I found a teller who wasn't busy, explained the situation to her, and gave her the ten thousand dollars. She went off and looked up Ambrose's account. When she came back, she made out a deposit slip and a duplicate and gave the latter to me. I left.

Ambrose was just approaching the front of the bank as I stepped out.

"What did you want to meet here for?" he asked.

"I have something which I have to give you," I said. I handed him the duplicate slip.

"Now I have to hurry. I have an appointment in a few minutes and then I'm leaving Reno in a couple of hours or so."

He squinted at the deposit slip. "What's this for?"

"It's a loan from me to you. For the mine. I think you may finally hit it rich, Ambrose. But you and your brother will need new equipment. That will help buy it. Put a big barrel in there and keep it filled with water. Buy a pump and you can use the water for sluicing. You can run the pump with a gasoline engine or with electricity. Along with the mine next to yours, you also get that big storage battery. Buy another as a backup. Then you will also have a fairly new machine for melting down the gold and making your own bricks."

"Why are you doing this, Milo?"

"You and Necktie were both helpful and I liked both of you. And you shouldn't have to work as hard as you do. If you get rich, you'll pay me back. If you don't, it's all right, too. The two of you helped me to earn that money, so it's only right that I use part of it to help you to earn more money. Now I have to go, Ambrose."

"Just one favor," he said. "Give me your address in New York. I might be able to repay you someday and I might want to write you a letter, even though I don't write so good."

I found a scrap of paper in my pocket and wrote it down

for him. He thanked me and I slapped him on the shoulder and then walked up the street to the Waldorf. It was about the right time, but Mei wasn't there yet. I sat on a stool at the end of the bar, and Joe came up and took my order for a martini.

"How's everything going?" he asked as he brought the martini.

"Good. I'm going back to New York this afternoon."

"Oh? You finished the case?"

"Yes."

"What about Dino?"

"He's in jail, and if he's smart he'll stay there for a while. Someone will be looking for him soon, and it won't be to give him a pat on the back. Dino was playing both ends against the middle. But he signed a release for me and I dropped my charges against him."

"Did your Chinese girl show up?"

"That's who I'm waiting for now. Tell one of the girls to save a table for me."

He nodded and left. I took a sip of my drink, found a dime in my pocket, and went to the phone back of me. I called the hotel and asked for Frank. There wasn't any answer, so I left a message saying that I was at the Waldorf and would be there for about an hour. I went back to the bar.

It was only about two sips later when the door opened and Mei walked in. She came over, gave me a kiss, and slid onto the stool next to me. She was carrying a shopping bag.

"I see you did some shopping," I said. "No cowboy hats, I hope."

She giggled.

I finished my drink and signaled to Joe to send back two drinks, and we went to the table. "What did you buy?" I asked her.

"Not much. A few little things to take back with me. Mostly Indian jewelry. That's all. How did it go with you?"

"Everything wrapped up. All we have to do now is have lunch, return the two cars I rented, figure out how to handle the Cadillac, check out, and get on a plane."

"I have already taken care of the Cadillac."

"How? Gave it to a local gangster?"

"No. It's already waiting to be shipped to New York. It'll be there in about a week and they'll phone you to pick it up when it arrives."

"Great," I said. "I love the Cadillac, honey, but what the hell do I do with a bullet-proof tank on Perry Street?"

"Drive it. Just the sight of it will probably help you to pick up all sorts of girls."

"I don't need all sorts of girls," I said. I became aware that somebody was standing beside our table. I looked up. It was Frank.

"Hello, Milo," he said. "Miss Hsu."

"Sit down and have a drink," I said.

"Can't have the drink. I'm on duty. But I will sit down for a minute. What's happened?"

"Not much. I got the release from Dino and his companions. I also advised him to stay in jail for a while. He'll be safer there until you pick up Bacci. I imagine that'll be sometime today or tonight."

He nodded. "We've added all the new charges against

Dino, and I think he'll get a nice, long vacation. We've also raided the first storage place for the gold bricks and arrested five men. The sixth one is probably at the new hiding place. You're sure Bacci will go there?"

"I'm sure. What about Carson City?"

"The three people are under arrest and the mine is staked out. And there is a connection to Dino. The girl worked for him in his house. And I have a paper for you to sign." He put it in front of me. I read it. Everything was all right about it. I signed it and handed it back to him.

"I just hope," he said, getting up, "that the Director doesn't find out how much work we're doing for you."

"Somebody," I said dryly, "should tell the Director to hire a gag writer to give you guys better lines."

He laughed. "Okay. Take it easy, Milo. Nice to have met you, Miss Hsu." He left.

We had our lunch and then we left. We walked down the street toward the LTD. Mei reached down and held my hand. It was a nice feeling. I wondered how much time we'd have at the hotel before we had to catch the plane.

A LAST GOODBYE

The last known snapshot of Ken Crossen and two obituaries conclude his last book published during his lifetime. They are mementos of a writer who provided pleasurable escapist reading for countless fans of the pulp, science fiction, mystery, and espionage, and detective genres. It's "a" last goodbye and not "the" last goodbye, as there is never a final goodbye to one who continues to live through his writings— and especially through the unforgettable character of Milo March.

Donald L. Miller, a publisher and editor of science fiction and mystery fanzines, produced a Ken Crossen issue of the *The Mystery Nook* (no. 12, June 1979), in which he reviewed the Milo March series. Because of a bout of illness that interrupted the project, he had to read the books over again when he resumed it. He writes: "I enjoyed almost all of the novels as much as, if not more than, I did the first time around. This is partially because I had forgotten so much after the first reading that it was almost like reading them for the first time the second time around. (Which is not a put-down—the series *is* trivial—but that works in its favor rather than against it. It is escape reading, pure and simple—the novels are all good, fast reads—each provides a couple of hours of entertainment, without lingering questions and after-thoughts.) But it was

Obituary

Feb. 3472
Kendall
Foster
Cr—

mostly because of my familiarity with March, an advantage enjoyed by most series over one-time appearance is the pseudo-bond which develops between the reader and the series character(s)."

Don also comments on the redundancy of Milo motifs: "His openly disrespectful bantering with Intercontinental Insurance's Martin Raymond, for example, and Raymond's idiotic reply, 'That's my boy!'; March's mandatory flirtation scene with each secretary in each new office he enters through each book; the mandatory nemesis March picks up early in each book; his credulity-defying effect on every pretty girl he

KENDELL FOSTER CROSSEN
JULY 25, 1910 -- NOVEMBER 29, 1981
(A delayed tribute written by Nick Carr)

HIS typewriter has been silent for some time. The days finally ran out for this gentle man I came to know more than just a friend. Ever slowly Death has plucked from the literary scene those who authored stories for the pulp magazines. Now we who remain behind try to pen a worthy epitaph and have trouble. Yet we must try because it helps to ease the pain within our own souls. Like Harold F. Cruickshank and Frederick C. Davis, this man Crossen had a way of putting words to a piece of paper and making his characters live. For some his literary people were bigger than life because Ken himself was a very meticulous and thorough guy in his research.

Perhaps what I'm trying to say is that Ken was a person who knew how to live and when the time came--knew how to die. To prove what I mean I am going to break a long standing rule and quote part of a letter I recieved from his wife, Marcelia: "You know that Ken has been sick for a very long time. He was released from this misery on Sunday, November 29th. His going was so peaceful that I can scarcely believe that he is gone." I think probably the real Ken Crossen was a composite between all of those characters found in his novels. I see him as Milo March, Insurance Investigator; as Lt. Col. Kim Locke, U.S. Army, on loan to the CIA; as Brian Brett, investigator for the Excelsior Insurance Company; as Jethro Dumont, the Green Lama. When I'd often call him up early in the morning, his usual response on the other end of the line was: "Good morning, I think." This wasn't really odd because I knew that was Milo March talking as Ken wasn't fully awake yet. But probably I will remember him like this: He sat in the easy chair rubbing his white beard with long, tapering fingers of the right hand. In his left a cigarette sent thin wisps of smoke drifting snakelike into the room. A probing shaft of morning sunlight gently touched a gold medallion he wore around his neck. What then shall his epitaph be? I've gone over our vast correspondence and for an old pulp buff like myself, there can be but one: It comes from a Green Lama story: "Then the lights flickered out and a shadowy figure slipped from the room. Behind him an eerie whisper seemed to echo: 'Om! Ma-ni pad-me hum!'

So sleep well, my friend, you who now write for the Gods!

encounters; the mandatory put-down of the military each time Milo has a run-in with it; and so on. The list of such irritants is quite long, and any one such irritant would be enough to ruin many a story. But, somehow, they only hurt the March novels if one sits back and thinks about them while reading

the novels. In fact, the cumulative effect of these irritants may be exactly the opposite from what one would expect—if one reads the novels quickly, in a relaxed atmosphere and without stopping to think about them along the way—as most escape reading should be and is read. These repeated irritants, plus the often-exaggerated stereotyping, plus the super-hero March character, produce a work that is almost parodic in nature. This near-parodic treatment then adds to the humor and makes the books even more enjoyable, rather than dragging the stories down as is the case with many full parodies."

Don Miller rates the twenty-one novels on a scale of 1 to 9, best to worst, giving one 2 *(The Man Inside),* eight 3's, six 4's, one 5, and one 9 *(Hangman's Harvest).* He concludes: "I did enjoy the series. A hard-nosed reviewer could really tear the books apart; but I read them for enjoyment, and enjoyment was what I got—what more can one ask from escape reading?"

Fortunately there are two more Milo March volumes in the Steeger Books series that didn't exist at the time of Don's reviews: *Death to the Brides*, written in 1975 and now published for the first time by Steeger Books, and *The Twisted Trap: Six Milo March Stories*, the first collection of short fiction starring our hero. Escape and enjoy.

Kendell Foster Crossen (1910–1981), the only child of Samuel Richard Crossen and Clo Foster Crossen, was born on a farm outside Albany in Athens County, Ohio—a village of some 550 souls in the year of this birth. His ancestors on his mother's side include the 19th-century songwriter Stephen Collins Foster ("Oh! Susanna"); William

Allen, founder of Allentown, Pennsylvania; and Ebenezer Foster, one of the Minute Men who sprang to arms at the Lexington alarm in April 1775.

Ken went to Rio Grande College on a football scholarship but stayed only one year. "When I was fairly young, I developed the disgusting habit of reading," says Milo March, and it seems Ken Crossen, too, preferred self-education. He loved literature and poetry; favorite authors included Christopher Marlowe and Robert Service. He also enjoyed participant sports and was a semi-pro fighter in the heavyweight class. He became a practicing magician and had a passion for chess.

After college Ken wrote several one-act plays that were produced in a small Cleveland theater. He worked in steel mills and Fisher Body plants. Then he was employed as an insurance investigator, or "claims adjuster," in Cleveland. But he left the job and returned to the theater, now as a performer: a tumbling clown in the Tom Mix Circus; a comic and carnival barker for a tent show, and an actor in a medicine show.

In 1935, Ken hitchhiked to New York City with a typewriter under his arm, and found work with the WPA Writers' Project, covering cricket for the *New York City Guidebook.* In 1936, he was hired by the Munsey Publishing Company as associate editor of the popular *Detective Fiction Weekly.* The company asked him to come up with a character to compete with The Shadow, and thus was born a unique superhero of pulps, comic books, and radio—The Green Lama, an American mystic trained in Tibetan Buddhism.

Crossen sold his first story, "The Aaron Burr Murder Case," to *Detective Fiction Weekly* in September 1939, but says he didn't begin to make a living from writing till 1941. He tried his hand at publishing true crime magazines, comics, and a picture magazine, without great success, so he set out for Hollywood. From his typewriter flowed hundreds of stories, short novels for magazines, scripts radio, television, and film, nonfiction articles. He delved into science fiction in the 1950s, starting with "Restricted Clientele" (February 1951). His dystopian novels *Year of Consent* and *The Rest Must Die* also appeared in this decade.

In the course of his career Ken Crossen acquired six pseud-onyms: Richard Foster, Bennett Barlay, Kent Richards, Clay Richards, Christopher Monig, and M.E. Chaber. The variety was necessary because different publishers wanted to reserve specific bylines for their own publications. Ken based "M.E. Chaber" on the Hebrew word for "author," *mechaber.*

In the early '50s, as M.E. Chaber, Crossen began to write a series of full-length mystery/espionage novels featuring Milo March, an insurance investigator. The first, *Hangman's Harvest,* was published in 1952. In all, there are twenty-two Milo March novels. One, *The Man Inside,* was made into a British film starring Jack Palance.

Most of Ken's characters were private detectives, and Milo was the most popular. Paperback Library reissued twenty-five Crossen titles in 1970–1971, with covers by Robert McGin-nis. Twenty were Milo March novels, four featured an insur-ance investigator named Brian Brett, and one was about CIA agent Kim Locke.

Crossen excelled at producing well-plotted entertainment with fast-moving action. His research skills were a strong asset, back when research meant long hours searching library microfilms and poring over street maps and hotel floorplans. His imagination took him to many international hot spots, although he himself never traveled abroad. Like Milo March, he hated flying ("When you've seen one cloud, you've seen them all").

Ken Crossen was married four times. With his first wife he had three children (Stephen, Karen, Kendra) and with his second a son (David). He lived in New York, Florida, Southern California, Nevada, and other parts of the country. Milo March moves from Denver to New York City after five books of the series, with an apartment on Perry Street in Greenwich Village; that's where Ken lived, too. His and Milo's favorite watering hole was the Blue Mill Tavern, a short walk from the apartment.

Ken Crossen was a combination of many of the traits of his different male characters: tough, adventuresome, with a taste for gin and shapely women. But perhaps the best observation was made in an obituary written by sci-fi writer Avram Davidson, who described Ken as a fundamentally gentle person who had been buffeted by many winds.

CPSIA information can be obtained
at www.ICGtesting.com
Printed in the USA
FSHW021648210521
81498FS

9 781618 275837